OUR DARK SECRET

A MODERN CUCKOLD MEMOIR

OUR DARK SECRET

A MODERN CUCKOLD MEMOIR

DERRIN HART

fannypress

Seattle, Wa

Published by Fanny Press
PO Box 70515
Seattle, WA 98127
All rights reserved. No part of this book may be reproduced or transmitted in any form or by any means, electronic or mechanical, including photocopying, recording, or any information storage and retrieval system, without permission in writing from the publisher.

Cover design by Sabrina Sun

Contact: info@fannypress.com

Copyright © 2010 by Derrin Hart

ISBN: 978-1-60381-485-0 (Paper)
ISBN: 978-1-60381-486-7 (ePub)

This is the true story of our "guilty pleasures."

Often the "guilt" involved is simply fear of others discovering one's doings, or otherwise embarrassing tastes, rather than actual moral guilt.

Prologue

One warm summer day my girlfriend Janet and I were relaxing on a beach blanket next to the Atlantic Ocean. The sun was shining and life was good. I had met Janet a few years earlier and we were planning on getting married one day. As young twenty-three year olds, life was ours for the taking. I was happy with my choices. Janet was a cute if not very sexy young woman. Today she had on a tiny yellow, orange and blue bikini. There was no denying that this little girl—a mere one hundred and five pounds—was a looker. She had frosted blond hair and a fabulous flat tummy. I, too, was not so bad. I was athletic and solid. Woman liked my looks and I was a manly man. Together we made a good couple and yes, we were in love.

I—for some unexplained reason—enjoyed watching the guys on the beach look at Janet. It was a great turn-on to see them glance over and, when she walked over to the water, gawk and lick their lips. Like most men, I could be jealous, but this aspect of "all eyes on my tiny girlfriend" just got to me. I never much thought about having any sort of open marriage or swinging lifestyle with her. We were young and very compatible.

Sexually we fit. For a couple years now we had made love a lot. Though in good shape and full of energy, I had a somewhat-small penis. However, Janet was a small thing and her vaginal opening was as tight as I had ever experienced in a woman. We connected well, the sex was good, and she was a "cummer"—orgasmic even with just straight intercourse. I loved it.

This story, at least most of it, is about me and my wife. Janet is not my wife. But to learn how my cuckold ways came about, I must start at the beginning. I am currently married; my bride Sara's long tale—*Our Dark Secret*—is yet to come. I was not a cuckold to begin with; I was a young, fun-seeking chap who just wanted to have a lot of sexual freedom. While visiting a local adult bookstore, I came across *Swinger Magazine*. These books got me thinking and the ads and pix made me wonder. I had never heard of such a thing, and with Janet I thought, *wow, we could get into this stuff*. I mean, after two years we needed some excitement; after all, I loved adventure.

That day, while we sat on a blanket enjoying the wonderful ocean view, I told Janet, "Babe, I think we should try swinging and couple swapping. We could meet men for you to have fun with."

Janet stared at me with her big brown eyes and replied, "What on earth are you talking about?"

Chapter One

One evening, weeks later, I was pushing my cock into Janet's tightness and she was moaning with pleasure. I could feel her walls gripping my small member. We became one, a perfect fit. She would explode in orgasm soon enough, and afterward we would snuggle side by side.

Janet kissed me softly and our eyes met. "I have been thinking about what you said at the beach, honey," she said, "and I guess, if it means a lot to you, we can try it out." I was nervous, not wanting her to freak out on it all, yet very excited by her words.

The next day I made my way to the porn shop and bought a *Swingers Magazine*. I spotted a new one, a local publication. I went to the counter, a little embarrassed yet intent on the purchase. The booklet was in black and white, not the big full-color format like some of the larger national magazines. However, it would do, and I left the shop with what was to become my intro the swinging lifestyle.

That evening Janet sucked my cock. She loved to suck cock. As usual, when we were ready enough to fuck, we used lubrication and that led to great sex. I kept thinking of the possibility that another guy might join us. How he would love her tight little body. What a gift she would be to an older gentlemen—a young, tight, sexy girl he could cherish. I was hard again in seconds after my own first climax. During our second joining we talked about placing an ad, and she came quickly again. God I loved a girl who could get off through just the screwing itself!

The booklet had space for placing an ad. I tore it out and filled in words. They read like this, "Tiny tight-bodied young girlfriend seeks an older lover. She is very attractive, toned and tanned. Boyfriend may watch or join in." We placed the ad, bought a post office box for replies and waited anxiously for good letters. This was all new to me. In those days there was no Internet, no way to meet anyone other than through these magazines. I also had the option to post a note on the adult bookstore wall. I worried someone we knew would answer the ad but decided to try it anyway.

The anticipation of attracting a respondent was wild. Janet and I had a good relationship. She was a good girl and I was the ring leader. I would never have thought of myself as a cuckold at this time in my life. I pretty much called the shots. We received a few replies in the coming months, but most were weird or from men who were overweight, too old, or wanted me— the male—to participate in full. I was by no means interested in going there. Eventually, though, one reply stood out that was worth pursuing.

William was his name. He was in his late forties, in decent shape, and seemed classy enough. The following weekend we made plans. I was to meet him in a nearby hotel parking lot, a place easy to find off the interstate. Janet would be home waiting for us. She would wear a sexy blue cami and matching string bikini panty. She would wait on our bed. Our plan was, if I liked the guy, he would come to our home and massage her. Where things would go from there, we had no clue. Thinking back, I can't imagine inviting a strange man to my now home. Sara would forbid it. Plus, it's downright dangerous. A hotel was the way to go. Yet, as a young foolish guy, I knew no better, had no funds for travel and nice hotel lodgings, and did not even know if this stuff would be right for me and my girl more than just this one time.

William and I hooked up; I saw his red car and drove up and got in. The parking lot was quiet, and we sat and talked. Here I was, speaking with a random stranger about coming to fondle and possibly fuck my young girlfriend. Man was I crazy, yet fully aroused.

He seemed nice, relaxed and easy going enough, so I had him follow me home.

When we got back, Janet was right where we planned, lying on the bed, face down. She looked awesome—so small yet firm, tan and sexy. He was very pleased. He sat and prodded her body, touching and massaging her completely. Few words were spoken.

Janet then turned over, more relaxed now. William slid his hands to her small perky breasts, a nice rounded upright 34B cup. He fondled her and touched her as I looked on. I joined in, and her excitement began to build. The idea of four hands on her body was intoxicating to me, and I was amazed to see it become a reality.

He slid a hand in her panties, and she was enjoying it. Soon enough we had her out of her outfit and fully nude on the bed. William, too, got undressed. This would be my first time seeing another in-the-flesh male naked in front of me and my lover, yet he would be one of many to come. He was decently in shape, but my eyes went right to his thick, uncut penis. He was hung well, and his foreskin covered what appeared to be a nice cock head. Janet had unzipped my pants and was sucking me already. William exposed her inner thighs and dropped down to lick her now-ready pussy. Janet had no outer pussy lips, just an opening—an opening so tight that even my smallish penis couldn't enter without lube. His saliva dashed about her and she groaned in pleasure.

This guy was in heaven. He was a near-fifty-year-old guy tasting a young twenty-three-year-old who was a looker. He had hit the jackpot. I loved having a fellow partner help me satisfy Janet. It was it easy to put her into sky-rocketing orbit. The stranger took no time between her legs; he grabbed her and made her kneel. He positioned himself behind her and wanted to enter immediately. She sucked me still and I watched as he mounted her backside, her tiny butt sticking up ready to receive him. I got a glimpse of his hard-on; he was big and rock stiff. She would take him deep and she looked right at me as he pushed in. I will never forget her face. She was like a deer in headlights; this large dong was one she had never experienced. His size opened her, and she looked at me with shock; yet her eyes began to glaze over once he was fully in. "Oh lord," she blurted out. "He's so big."

I looked at this stranger who now had my foxy girlfriend in a frenzy. Then it happened way too fast; he could not hold off, and he pulled out, spurting his white goo all over her ass. She was too tight for him, too fresh, too young. This very pretty girl had made him cum in less that one minute. In those days I would take over, fuck my girl and make her cum. This was just the beginning, however. In time, when my bride Sara and I took to this lifestyle, things would be very different.

Janet and I planned a few more events in the coming months. We tried a couple in which the female half was a hottie. The girls pranced about for us guys, drinking margaritas and modeling various outfits. The guy in the couple was a good-looking, younger body-builder type. As the night progressed we all joined in on the floor for some fun. I was turned on by him being with Janet, but his girl wanted me. This was my first lesson in what I truly desired, and it was not another woman. I could not get hard. She commented on me being small in size, and Janet was over there sucking her guy hard and wanting more. I just wanted to watch my little sexpot go at it.

Those two encounters had set me off. Normal sex would not do anymore. I wanted my girl to have it all—meaning more men, multiple men if need be. We really did not need couples or women; I wanted men for her. Our sex life had taken a dive, so generic it had become. I found myself wanting more. It had taken a toll on us. But we still were doing fine and decided a year later to get engaged. Janet was my girl, a small-town poor kid who followed my lead. She was good looking, and men turned their heads when she passed by. I was happy and we made plans for our future.

    I made it a point to update the ad we had placed, this time with a picture. Who could resist this tiny woman with perky breasts and abs of steel? With such a picture we got many replies. In today's swinging world, the online aspect is truly awesome. These paper ads and letters via regular mail were a major pain. The quality of people seeing a porn store booklet ad sucked. However, we carried on.

Chapter Two

One guy who we invited to our apartment arrived with Kentucky Fried Chicken buckets. Another appeared completely different from his picture. Both were way below Janet's standards, which were not overly high as long as the guys were attractive and nice. These two were plainly average—if that. The balding second guy was aggressive, and when I was in the bathroom, he pushed Janet over and penetrated her before I was back in the room. I suddenly realized something: none of these people were using condoms.

Months went by and we had our first big scare. Janet might be pregnant; she was late for her period. This took a toll on us—a big toll. Luckily she started again a week later. More replies to our ad came in and I found one most interesting. He was older, as everyone was compared to us. He looked attractive enough and claimed to have ten inches. I was starting to get into this whole size thing. All the men we met were bigger than me. Janet seemed to like it and I was really turned on by her taking a huge cock. This big guy was our next guest.

I decided we'd have a little extra fun this time too. I bought a video camera and came up with a role-playing scenario, even though Janet was feeling overwhelmed by the idea of role-playing. Tim arrived on cue and the scene was set in motion. Janet wore a tiny black dress, thigh-high black stockings and heels. She wore no panties and no bra. He was a traveling insurance salesman who had arrived at our door. I had a good imagination. He entered while giving us his sales pitch.

Janet soon had him sit on the couch to discuss our buying options. She interrupted him, saying, "My boyfriend was supposed to be here. I'm sorry he's running late. He's always late. We had dinner plan after this and dancing ... very disappointing."

Tim was on her side, of course. He said, "I find it hard to imagine any guy being late for you. I mean, you're such a little darling if I may say so."

Janet blushed and they chatted more. He flirted with her and played up what he was selling, moving in closer and after a while massaging her shoulders. The role-playing proceeded on its own. I just watched and filmed.

He offered to take her to the bedroom, and she agreed. In our room he undressed her and ate her pussy with reckless abandon. She was loving it and moaning louder each minute he indulged her. She said, "Oh please, fuck me. Please give it to me." I was like, wow, she is really into this. Has she had too many wine coolers? She sat up, undid his pants, and the little cocksucker went to town. Tim was not hung. He had six inches, not ten. I was wholly disappointed. He had lied. He took my girl and fucked her. She loved it, but I was upset the entire time.

We took a break after that sad meeting. It seemed like this whole setup had disappointment written all over it. These guys were porn-shop-booklet readers. I mean, what did we expect? In the future the Internet would change all this. But not before Janet and I tried more encounters. Things would soon come crashing down on our engagement.

We invited another older guy to join us in the bedroom about six months later.

Janet wore a sexy red dress and white stockings. She furiously sucked his smallish cock, which his letter had claimed was bigger. He was not hard throughout. He wasted no time stripping her down, sliding her panties off and eating her pussy. She was on fire, but he could not get hard. They tried everything with no luck. We invited another guy over months later. He was a heavy-set guy but carried a thick cock.

Janet sucked him good. He was stiff and had a big mushroom cockhead.

Before this meet-up we had discussed the aspect of condom-less sex. We could not keep taking chances. We bought some condoms, but they stayed in the drawer. She climbed her little butt on top of him, looked back at me with wanting eyes and mounted him. She rode his fat dick and loved it. The coming weeks we were scared as hell again about her being pregnant. It was killing us.

Then another major obstacle came up. Janet became obsessed with the subject of sexually transmitted diseases. Here we were having her screw random men, condom-less, unprotected and bare. Not only was she in danger, but so was I. She decided we had to stop all swinging.

At the time I was teaching at a nearby school. Out of the blue a new student walked in. She was a sixteen-year-old bushy-blond baby doll named Sara. Janet met her at a gathering and immediately did not like her. It was a jealousy thing. Anyway, life went on. Little did I know my future wife had just stepped into my world.

Years past. We met a few other guys, no one special. We mostly dealt with one another and what life was sending our way.

Things in my life were changing fast. The little girl I had loved as a high school junior was still my best pal and lover. However, the sex was getting stale, and our swinging was on hold. I was wary of diseases from the past encounters, and even got ill at one point. I thought I may have AIDS—the latest scare in the modern world of the nineties.

I still wanted more wild sexy adventures, but none came about for quite a long time. Janet and I were facing typical relationship woes. Finances were low, our jobs not what we wanted, and she was constantly talking marriage and children. I was leery of a lot. I did not know where things were heading. I hated all this stuff. We needed a house, better jobs, more money—not to mention more exciting sex. We also had to deal with Janet's family.

Oh boy, what a messed up crew! She was the baby of eight kids. Most were alcoholics, and her closest-aged sister was the worst. We had a fight one night about all the above and Janet left. Her sister encouraged her to leave. But Janet came back crying into my arms and we made amends. Again money was tight. Janet wanted marriage and she wanted a child. Swinging was not on her list. I began fantasizing about other women, just to get by sexually. I was a young teacher and students were but a mere six to seven years my junior, so these lovely girls were great fodder for fantasy.

I did not want a child yet, and marriage scared the hell out of me. I knew only one true girlfriend. Janet and I never had reason to imagine we would not be together forever.

She wanted more and wanted it now. I asked that we swing more, perhaps meet some hot men—not the duds we had met before. The Internet was now an option and more possibilities were soon to come. Janet lost her job. We had little money, and we fought more and more. Her sister missed her, and she her sister. We split again, but she came running back into my arms. "I love you," she insisted. "You and me are all I have."

It looked like we'd be okay. Still, once I was feeling good again, I got lost in the subject that would destroy us. I wanted Janet to be with a black man. My soon-to-be wife was thinking wedding, a child and a new job. Again we had to split. This time she would not return. She had always come back, but this time Janet had met someone at her new job. He had been her friend in a time of need. He was nothing special but he cared. Together they would talk, him telling her how he would cherish her beyond reason. He would tell her I was a fool.

I still thought she'd be back. I wanted to marry her and I did want a child someday. We'd been together for many years and we'd met right out of school. We were always together. A week later a big argument ensued on the phone: "I suppose we could get together and talk," she said. I was like, "how could you be with another guy?" She was mad. "It didn't seem to bother you when we met those older guys before." I argued that this was different, but she could not see the difference. We didn't have that meeting until much later in the month.

The time spent alone was new to me. Janet and I was all I had ever had. I missed her and had a hard time imagining life without her. I was hurt, but I also felt guilty. She'd be back.

She did not come back. I was on my own and we corresponded very little for weeks. One day, while I was shopping and at the checkout line, I ran into a student from quite a ways back. She was gorgeous. I knew that bushy blonde hairstyle from far away. Her name was Sara and I was in awe. She came up to me and gave me a hug. It had been so long, and she was no longer a teenager. We chatted, and I suggested we should get together for a movie or something. She smiled and said, "Just give me a call sometime." Before I could say more, she had left the store. She was all paid up, and I was still dealing with the cashier.

I heard nothing from Janet in the coming days. I thought about calling Sara, but it was mostly a fantasy. I did not have her number and she was a lot younger. Yet she did say that her boyfriend and she had recently split. I called Janet instead. She was a little easier to talk with, but we got nowhere with regard to meeting or getting back together. Then came a luck-of-the-draw, spur-of-the-moment happening: I ran across some old papers with student numbers from long ago and such. The papers were for a carwash we had done as a group years ago. They were listed on the back of something, since I hadn't thought it important to save the numbers. There stood one number in particular, Sara's.

This young woman was no doubt out of my league. She was slim, beautiful, young, and a college coed. Sara could be a playboy playmate in an instant. I fidgeted with the number for two days and only got the nerve to call on a Wednesday night. She was back home from school, and luckily her mother passed her the phone. "Hi, Sara. After running into you at the store, I decided to call. How about we hit a movie together this Friday night?" My heart was pounding out of my chest. Janet was on my mind. What the heck was I doing?

Sara calmly answered my call. "I'd love to."

Chapter Three

Our first date was good. We saw a fun movie and ended up back at my apartment.

Sara was different than Janet. She was a modern woman—more independent. Janet was a good looking girl, if not cute. Sara was a doll. Her teeth were perfect and white as snow, her thick blonde mane ever flowing and splendid. She had high cheekbones and a face of an angel. We talked for hours and got along real well. I had a young-for-my-age outlook on life. Hers seemed to match.

I told her we should get together again. She agreed, and we shared a nice hug before I took her home. The following week, on Monday morning, we hooked up again. As we walked alongside a lovely pond, we talked about life, the future and whatnot. Sara and I had connected. We were going to have another date. I just knew it.

That afternoon Janet finally called me. She wanted to meet. We made plans and met up beside a nearby lake. We sat on an up-rise of rocks and had our first serious talk since the split. Janet was her old self. She mentioned that things have been crazy, and I agreed wholeheartedly. We looked into each other's eyes and all we had shared flashed before me. We had been inseparable for years. She was a great girl. Life—yes, life—had just thrown us a serious curveball. "Maybe we should get back together,' she said. "What about John?" I said. I then mentioned that I, too, had been seeing someone. She cried, as did I. We decided that we'd wait, see how things progressed. Janet and I never did get back together.

As mentioned earlier, as a young man my first experience with swinging and cuckold material came at the adult bookstore in a nearby town. I was getting magazines every so often there, the types that showed real sex with real couples. I really liked the images of well-endowed men with sexy ladies. One day I saw an image on the cover of a magazine that was called *Cocoa and Cream* and decided to give it a try. I bought the magazine.

    I hadn't realized that this magazine was a swingers book. I figured it was like most others, but in truth, it was the beginning of my desire for interracial cuckold fun. These ads said things I never imagined I would consider. Sexy wives were seeking black men for sex. Husbands were said to enjoy watching, and the ads claimed to be real. I enjoyed the ads and never really thought twice about their meaning until my twenties had passed me by. My thirties had arrived, and this book remained with me in my most private bedroom drawer.

    How could I consider such forbidden action? I mean, why would I let a woman I loved, or liked for that matter, be intimate with another man again? Now, at the age of thirty-three, I had a chance meeting with a gal I had known earlier. Luckily for me, she was single. I asked her on a date. She was a stunning blonde, ripe at the age of twenty-two. I always had a thing for blondes. This doll looked a lot like the typical Barbie doll I so admired. I saw her as a Pamela Anderson type, though a country girl with a gorgeous set of teeth, vibrant smile, and a welcoming attitude. Sara was her name. She had a wonderful curvy body, and the type of hair you usually only found on Hollywood starlets.

    Now that I was older, I wondered if we would hit it off and find a connection that could last. Well, we did and have been married ever since. Never in my wildest dreams would I have conceived what we would do and go through in the years to come. This is our story, our "Dark Secret."

    Sara, my new wife, was not the stuck-up type. She was and is down to earth and very artsy. We began dating and really got along well. She is needy in many ways. She likes to be told she is special and enjoys the admiration. I had no problem with obliging her. She seemed very sexual when we first touched, and her body was great. She stands five foot five and weighs about one hundred and twenty five pounds. Her breasts are a shapely 34c cup. She kept in good shape and at that time she was a young beautiful coed. I stole her from the college boys, and that was no easy feat.

Before we got married we talked about all her experiences in high school and college. Surprisingly, she had had sex with many guys in college. At first I was shocked. In high school, she only had one boyfriend. She claimed that being alone and away from her family in college had made her seek out love and companionship. I think she spoke the truth, yet I also think the new freedom and partying had something to do with it. She obviously did enjoy it; ten guys is a lot of screwing for a one-boyfriend high school chick. Sex and penetration came easy to Sara.

Our story really begins in 1996. While still dating, we finally had sex and right away I was dumbfounded when I entered her. I could penetrate each of my past girlfriends decently but always with the help of lubrication. Sara was very wet, and I slid in without any friction at all. As we copulated she became even more open and soon I could not feel her walls; my penis was lost inside her. This small college girl had an opening and wetness that engulfed me, and I was bedazzled.

This was the first time I came to realize I had a rather small penis. Plus, she had a generous vaginal opening. According to my reading in the *Kama Sutra*, we were not well matched. According to the *Kama Sutra*, the ancient Indian Hindu sex text, a man and woman are divided into three sexual organ classes. Men can be classified as hare men, bull men and horsemen, according to the size of his cock. Women, too, can be classified as does, mares or female elephants, depending on the depth of their cunts. There are three equal unions that can exist between a man and a woman, depending on their sizes, and six unequal ones.

The equal matches are hare and doe, bull and mare, and horse and elephant. It was obvious my college girl and I were not equally matched. I was over six feet tall and outweighed her considerably, but our organs were way off.

In unequal unions, when the male exceeds the female in size, his union with a woman who is immediately next to him in size is called high union and is of two kinds; his union with the woman farthest from his size is called the highest union, and is of one kind only. On the other hand, when the female exceeds the male in size, her union with a man immediately next to her in size is called low union, and is of two kinds; her union with a man farthest from her in size is called the lowest union, and is of one kind only. In other words, the horse/mare and bull/deer form the high unions, while the horse/deer union is the highest. On the female side, the elephant/bull and mare/hare form low unions, while the elephant/hare union is lowest. There are, then, nine kinds of unions based on dimensions. Equal unions are the best; those of a superlative degree, i.e., the highest and the lowest, are the worst. The rest are middling, and with them the high are better than the low.

We managed the best we could with such a low union throughout our courtship year. But after awhile I came to realize that sex with Sara was difficult and unfulfilling for both of us. What could we do to change this? I could not help think of my past with Janet. But this relationship was nothing like my prior youthful one. Sara was a very independent young woman. A modern girl, educated and heading for a successful international career.

I finally decided to explore swinging with her. I raised the possibility of another man—a stud—joining us. At first she was stunned, saying she would be frightened and uneasy. I had an old buddy coming to town one weekend and mentioned he could be a good choice to start with. I also began looking for swinger parties in our rural neck of the woods, seeing if maybe something local would also be an option. We planned the old buddy encounter and I even bought a new video recorder. Sara was so nervous, yet she felt a twinge of excitement. So we decided to go ahead with our plans. Sara had not been raised to be a swinger, much less have encounters with other people while in a relationship. She was extremely apprehensive.

 I laid her lingerie out on the bed before our friend was to arrive. We had decided she would do a little modeling show for him and I, and we picked out five special outfits. She looked so amazing. She had painted her finger- and toenails red and was brushing her gorgeous long blonde hair as I stepped out to pick our man up at the airport. He was a white guy, although my mind's eye kept seeing our fantasy man as colored. The thing was, there really were no black men to speak of in our state.

 I had not seen John in a while and when we met, I was a little disappointed. He had aged not as well as I had hoped. He was slightly balding and his body was average. This guy used to be well built and good-looking. But time changes all, so off we went back to our apartment to meet Sara. Introductions were made, and she prepared to come out in her outfits for us. Wow, was I fully turned on by the thought of this guy seeing my girl partially nude and looking so fabulous! I think he was, too. My cock stiffened in my pants, and my balls tightened. He mentioned how gorgeous she was and that I was a very lucky man.

 Well, she came out and danced and paraded about for us. It was a moment to remember. Gorgeous and so lovely are two words that come to mind. She was nervous but did okay and changed into all five outfits like a good girl. She modeled long sheer negligee gowns, naughty two-piece biker bras and panties, even soft delicate pink baby doll camisoles. All these changes were amazing. With each one she seemed more relaxed. A massage followed, and John was more than happy to offer his hands. Sara was shaking. I had blindfolded her and told her to relax and lie on her stomach. She wore a tiny light blue cami and thong panty for the massage, and John wasted no time caressing every inch of her. In truth, she was way superior to him in looks. He would have had no chance with her other without this golden opportunity I gave him.

After a bit, he touched her in places inappropriate in a regular massage. She seemed to like it. Eventually he removed her lingerie, and the two started in on some sexual play. He ate her and she opened up for more. I noticed his cock was not all that big and was disappointed. Yet it was hard and she was anxious to have it. She got on top to start and slipped him in with one thrust. She rode him hard and moaned and arched repeatedly. "Oh yes, this feels so good!" she cried out. Things were going well, and I heard her say, "Please turn me over and fuck me like a dog." He positioned her on her knees and was all excited but regretfully came after just a few humps.

That was pretty much the end of our first encounter. She admitted afterward that he was not all that attractive to her and that she probably should have not gone further with sexual play. However, horny was horny, and she had wanted to make me happy by going all the way.

After that we dropped the swinging idea for a few months. I would not call it a great first experience. Sara was raised catholic, and her guilt lingered for some time.

Chapter Four

Our relationship was great. Sara and I had a lot in common. We loved sports, dining, movies, the same type of music, and many other things. We had sex often enough to be happy, yet the matching was still off. After one session when I gave her my best shot—a long hard fucking that left me fully drained—she still desired more. Her words after I came would linger in my mind: "I want more. I want it harder, I like it deep. It makes me feel like a woman." Here I was—a budding cuckold—with this wholesome and gorgeous blonde coed. What the hell was I going to do?

I had found a party in a nearby city, so we decided to give that a try later in the year. Sara was hesitant, but said, "Why not?" We planned our first party trip that spring. The night before the party, I watched as she chose her outfit. This was a highlight for me and a major turn-on. Many people would be looking at her the following evening, and her choices were fantastic. I loved seeing her change; her protruding pussy lips were so big I could see them each time she switched panties, and her eraser-tip nipples stood out as well. I imagined another male or female touching her and making her happy. The party was the next night and chances were that something would happen.

For the party she picked a black dress, high black boots, and black nylon stockings. The time had come for us to head out. We had no idea what to expect, and she was very nervous. We arrived safely and the house was big enough to be comfy for all attendees. It was a couple's party, so the couples mingled. We were having fun and meeting a few nice couples. We had been given a tour of the private rooms upstairs when we arrived. Two couples were playing in one, and a guy with a large, semi-hard cock walked right by us. *Man, would Sara go wild with that thing*, I thought.

Later we met a couple who were both physical therapists—a classy, fun pair. This was a good thing for Sara, because she liked seeing professional couples enjoying freedom of sexual exploration. We did not hook up with anyone that night, but later, when the couple we had become friends with had several people fondle their female half, we got in on that. Having this professional, sexy, attractive wife enjoy hands all over her had turned my Sara on. I was glad we attended this party. Later at home Sara and I fucked, and she said that the party was fun, and she thought that maybe—just maybe—she'd like to attend more.

We would make love as much as possible in the months following the party. Sara was creative and wanted to try many positions. The thing was, we had a hard time in some. I could barely have her ride me; her curvaceous round ass sank deeply on me and my tiny dick was lost. We also tried side-spooning, but again her protruding bubble ass, a shapely round ball was in the way. I could not reach in enough. Life was good, though, and we got engaged. There was no way I was letting this girl get away. She graduated from college, and we were happy.

Halloween came, the party scene looked good. An out-of-state bash seemed best for us. We met a couple who wanted to attend such a costume party and made plans to make the trip together. Halloween is always a great time to dress up and become someone else. Sara was excited about that and looking forward to the party. I had done a little research and learned that both couples and single men attended them. *This might be our first opportunity to meet a black guy*, I thought. That really had been my fantasy all along. With a built black man, we would both have the best possible time, her playing and me watching. Plans were made and the party fast approached. The couple we had met prior to that at a restaurant was really nice. But I really had no interest in a couple at this point. Our sex life needed a serious infusion, a hung stud who could turn my girl on and fuck her for long hours, deeply and passionately.

We tried so hard to have good sex, but it was tough. I was small, she was large, and penetration was unfulfilling. We did our best, but in time I came to avoid sex whenever possible. I would masturbate frequently while thinking of my beautiful wife with another man. I envisioned a guy who would bang her silly to get off, using magazine pics, porn or whatnot. Most nights I would take pics of Sara and then place pics of so-called well-built men next to them and jerk off while fantasizing the two together.

One night we went out with the couple who would be attending the party with us and joining us on the three hour drive out of town. The female half was a blonde as well and a live wire. She truly liked men, and Sara fed off her energy. One night we went to a strip club, and the crowd was paying more attention to our ladies than the strippers on stage. We were asked to leave, for God's sake. One the way home we made a detour to park and let the ladies play in the back of the Dodge van. Soon the guy in the couple got involved, but it was hard to see the back seat action. He was older, and although Sara was horny, she wasn't overly into it. But we got along well with them and were looking forward to the big party in a few weeks. The couple teased Sara; they nibbled on her tits and fingered her pussy. The frolicking was interesting, nothing less or more—just a little back seat fun. The other wife Lainy was a firecracker. She and Sara were becoming friends, and this led to more anticipation regarding the upcoming party.

The Halloween bash had arrived and we were excited, to say the least. We had picked out some cool costumes. Sara wore a purple, see-through cat suit with black panty and bra and an eye mask. The couple we had made friends with were fine with the long drive, and we got hotel rooms together. The party was packed, and everyone was having a good time. The room was filled with crazy sexy costumed people. I had made it a point to contact a single black guy via an ad in the area where the party took place. He showed up, and when we did an intro, I knew Sara liked what she saw. We danced and she paraded about for a while. The two of them danced together once, too. She was very excited. He was very dark skinned, tall, and well-built. Unfortunately he ended up disappearing later on. She had been hoping to hook up with him, but we never did find him. So overall the party was okay. I had come to realize that she was excited over being with a black guy. Chances were we'd try again.

Later that night we talked more about black men, and she admitted she had dated one in college. I was taken aback by that. Here's this straight-laced Catholic blonde beauty from a non-black community who goes to school and beds a black guy!

In time we planned another out-of-state trip so Sara could take her board exams. We found a young, sexy black guy not to far from the hotel where we were going to stay and made arrangements for him to come by our suite the night we were there. Sara returned to the suite late that evening after a long exam day, but was still up for a meeting. She jumped in the shower and acted excited enough. Her outfit was hot. She had a light brown button down shirt—almost an off-white—a long, shapely black skirt, garter belt and stockings and a set of heels. Her long, thick, curly blonde hair cascaded down her shoulders and back. I knew we were in for one hell of a night.

The first meeting with a black man for sex had arrived. Sara was very nervous. I made my way to the lobby as she finished getting ready. I paced about wondering what the hell I was doing. He showed up in a black leather coat and slacks. He was bald, dark skinned, and rather young. I knew she would find him attractive. He seemed nice enough, a little cocky, yet likeable, so we headed up to our hotel room.

Sara was pacing about, but when we walked in, her face lit up. She liked what she saw. The night was about to get hot. The two chatted some and she would not make the first move. He finally called her to him and they embraced. He had her turn around so he could admire her look and figure. He even lifted her skirt up to see her booty. Her garter belt and black nylons made her look so sexy. She looked over at me and I'll never forget that look. She was like, *holy shit, I can't believe this is happening.* She said to me, "I am so horny, honey, oh my God!" He liked her round butt. He told her it stuck out like a peach. Soon he began to undress her. "Now this is an ass. Wow, nice booty!" They kissed passionately. I thought, *oh no, we never came up with any boundaries here.* The kissing part probably should have been a "no," yet I could do nothing to stop it now. Later on in our meetings this would become a serious issue, as you will soon see.

He slowly undid her bra and caressed her thick nipples. Then he laid her on the bed and licked her stomach until he had made his way to her groin area. Sliding her black panties to the side her tongued her thighs first, then slid into her already moist outer pussy lips. She was already moaning and ready. Licking her cunt now and fondling her breasts, he had gotten Sara so excited that she slid his pants off and played with his cock. She was giving head to a stranger in our hotel room! My cock got hard watching. I would soon find out that when she gives head, she really likes the guy. This would become a telltale sign she was not only turned on by the encounter but by the guy himself. Afterward they fucked. He had her in the missionary position, and she took him very easily. He was decent-sized but not big. Early in their copulation she got on top, and I heard her say, "I could fuck you all night long." They then did it doggie style, followed by him on top again. He soon came while she egged him on, saying, "I want you to cum, yes, cum hard, explode!" Luckily she made him wear a condom. After it all ended, I breathed a sigh of relief he had not cum in her without protection.

Our first ever black-man encounter would be one of many—some amazing and some not so good. In my head I would often hear her voice, "I want more. I want it harder, I like it deep. It makes me feel like a woman!"

I was horny as hell and asked if I could have her before we went to bed. She agreed, and I mounted her and came in minutes.

We got married. Years passed. As this memoir continues, we would meet some very well hung black men and one she would fall for big-time. This lifestyle would have its ups and downs and cause some dangerous relationship issues. At times we'd meet men she'd turn down; then she'd swear never to meet other men again. We'd try couples and girls, all on the road to swinging adventure. Me and my lovely blonde baby doll Sara.

Before the book proceeds any further, I want to say that I love my wife. These were not random, fun activities. Each time we went out I was as nervous as she. I watched over her like a hawk. She is my only true love. Each and every time we met someone, we were both very nervous about the encounter. I have posted personals and profiles that received a thousand replies. For the record we turned down nearly all of them, so when we did meet someone there was a lot of pressure for the encounter to be a success. Sara made a big commitment to try and make the hook-up good, but the anxiety for both of us was very high.

So, in essence this is the true story of a husband and the woman he loves. I was a modern cuckold, finding men to satisfy my wife. I would do whatever it took to make it work, to make her happy.

In bed, each time we'd fuck, I felt small and could sense Sara wanting more. I would go as deep as I could, but when I'd pull out to change positions her vagina would let out a quaff or air. I thought she was farting or something until I did a little side research. An air pocket occurs when built up air in the vagina shoots out. She had so much more room in there that, as small as I was, she had built-up air to release. It was crazy. My girlfriend Janet from many years in the past could hardly take my little penis. We constantly needed lube. My bride had extra space. She was not a very big girl in body size, and this was all new to me. I'd have to do my best to hold my ground.

While the benefits are obvious to the hot wife in a cuckold relationship, never think that the cuckold husband isn't getting something very special out of the arrangement. The typical cuckold enjoys much more than merely watching his lovely wife treated to a thick, juicy cock. He knows he can't please her and so is being realistic, pragmatic and extremely understanding. He offers the gift of his masculinity up so that she might enjoy sex as she should. It takes a selfless and devoted husband or lover to become a cuckold, but the benefits are amazing. He has a stunt cock to take care of his beloved.

To my mind, the cuckolding lifestyle should add sexual excitement and satisfaction to the marriage and provide an outlet for the husband's submission and the wife's dominance. The wife should remain *mostly* emotionally distant from her lovers. We were married now and had a lot to lose if these wild adventures went wrong. I would do my best to make good choices.

Another Halloween party opportunity came about later that year. Sara a huge fan of dressing up in costume attire, and agreed to a trip out of state to the party, and we planned an October bash that fall.

She thought a party and perhaps another sexy black man sounded fun. After all, the last encounter had gone well enough and she was ready for more. We would attend this party alone, and so booked a reservation at the hotel where the gathering would take place. She would dress as a sexy French maid and had an outfit of black silk and white lace material, stockings, heels and the works. She would also bring along a black sheer cat suit in case she felt like changing at any time during the evening.

    The hotel was a nice one, and the French maid and her butler made their way to the event room. It was exciting seeing couples dressed up sexy in the halls of the hotel. A few made sure to say hi. The men, of course, were eying Sara up and down. I know they were thinking that maybe later, after mingling a while, they might very well get together with us. But my idea of a good night would be finding a hot guy for the wife. I preferred to be in that scenario and only watch.

    We arrived in the main room and grabbed a table. Soon enough we were meeting people—mostly couples. We did meet a football type player, a rugged black guy who sat with us early in the evening. He dressed well—in a gangster pinstriped suit—and I felt he might be a great choice for later on. However Sara spotted a basketball-player type black guy who was also well dressed in a suit, with a mafia-like top hat on. So we made sure to mingle with him as well. Problem was he was already sitting with a couple—a dark haired slim beauty and her much older hubby.

    This night was about to get interesting. I pointed out both the black guys to a friendly woman dressed as a cowgirl, and she mentioned that she knew them rather well. She had been with both of them before at previous parties. She assured us that both were good in bed and well-mannered. Sara again really was only interested in the slimmer, taller fellow. As the music blasted in the big room, I convinced her to dance with the larger guy; perhaps a spark would ignite. Here they were: this interracial couple, my wife the young blond white girl and this big strong rugged black man dancing together. I was shaking some and watching out of the corner of my eye from my place near the doorway exit. I mean there are no black people—let alone big, handsome strong black men—where we live.

Well the dancing got my wife loosened up a little. Surprisingly, a few songs later, she entered a little dance-off for ladies. Wives danced on stage and the crowd cheered for the ones they liked best. Sara was getting loose; the crowd roared for her dancing. After a few too many drinks, she was feeling tipsy and almost fell off the stage, banging into a speaker; I was shaking my head and laughing. Girls were lifting their skirts and teasing the crowd. My wife showed her butt once and I liked the view. I loved seeing her round bubble ass available for all to see. I would do all I could as a loving cuckold to make this night end well.

I made my way to the leaner black guy and we talked. I told him Sara was interested. He said he was flattered and found her sexy and beautiful, yet he was with another couple that evening. He had promised to service the wife and did not want to renege; they were his regulars and his commitment was to her. The raven-haired lady was hot, I'll admit, and I'm sure she needed great black-bull fucking, as her hubby looked a step below her needs for sure. I told Sara the bad news, and she was very disappointed. We mingled some more, but there were no other good candidates as playmates for her. We decided to head back to our suite.

After attending this party and many others, I began to notice how many of these party couples are upper class. Swingers tend to travel a lot, dress sexy, and spend freely. Only the upper echelon of couples could afford the lifestyle. We were running with upscale folk these days.

Anyway, earlier, before we called it a night, I made sure to tell Kenny, the larger football player type, that we would soon be heading up to our suite. He should come up now or perhaps make a pass at Sara beforehand. Yet, as we exited, he was nowhere to be found. We left the party empty handed. I had overheard there were hospitality rooms upstairs where people could go to play with others sexually or watch at no charge. I had never heard about this sort of stuff and made a mental note to mention it to my wife when we got back to our suite.

She had been drinking and that made her horny, yet she had no one to play with. I asked her if she would be interested in checking out these playrooms. Sara contemplated the idea. Soon she changed into her sheer see-through black cat suit and said, "Let's go." So off we headed to one of the rooms. Under her cat suit, she had on a black bra and thong panty. Overall she looked incredible, sexier than ever, but for what? I was dumbfounded, with no idea where we could get sex for her. I was certainly not going to provide the long deep pounding I knew she had been craving the whole trip. As an older man, I was starting to lose my erections more and more, and being of small size to begin with made for rough going with such a fertile young passionate sex-child as Sara was becoming. She possessed a large set of pussy lips and a canal that welcomed thickness and pleasure that I could not provide. I could only hope we would find someone to help.

The room was small and a few wives were taking it on the beds from the small number of black and even fewer white men as we arrived. Sara was hot-looking, and many took note. One white guy commented on her as she was bending over, trying to get the radio to play some upbeat modern songs. He was like, "Holy shit, wow, very nice."

But there was no one she liked in the room. She was turned on but, as always, fussy as hell. Luckily Kenny showed up in the hallway outside, and I grabbed him, asking if he wanted to play. He looked like a guy in a suit ready to be drafted by the National Football League. He was a rugged stocky one for sure. He loved the idea of playing with sexy little Sara. Sara noticed us and came over. The three of us headed to our own room; it looked like we had an encounter unfolding. She was horny and he was decent enough looking, so she agreed.

To give them a chance to get acquainted on the couch in the suite room, I hid in the bathroom down the hallway. Then I heard her call out to me to come watch. I sat nearby in a chair. As they embraced, I felt a stirring in my loins. She was soon hot; he got up and quickly took off his clothes. He was well-hung and thick, and I knew she would have it good. They moved to the bed and she slipped out of the sheer cat suit.

She did not suck him off. I kind of figured that would be the case. But he ate her good, and she was moaning and enjoying the cunt lapping. Soon he mounted her and she said, "Oh my God," as her entered her. He was a big guy and began pounding her steadily; she took him fully with ease. He lifted her legs over her shoulders and slammed into her. Sara yelped out, "Holy shit, oh my lord, yes, yes, give it to me, fuck me baby!" She screamed in ecstasy, loudly and wildly, and he came with a groaning grunt.

After he left I asked if I could have her. She was tired but agreed; I mounted her and came in minutes. She mentioned how she had not been overly attracted to him, but had just been horny. We left it at that. The following morning he called to say he wanted more, but Sara was not interested. He told me on the phone he had been with the cowgirl before us. He apologized, saying the cowgirl had given him head in the elevator, but that next time he would be at full throttle for lovely Sara.

There would not be a next time with him. That morning, as we headed home, the drive was quiet. It would be a long time before we found anyone new for my wife.

I began thinking, what is a cuck, really? During the first black-stud encounter, I had watched without touching, knowing that later I would have the opportunity to clean up her sore and well-used pussy. I marveled at her capacity for pleasure, knowing it far outdid my own. She deserves to have it fully deep and long lasting. We could do better, I thought. There were men out in the world that could give her great pleasure and send her skyrocketing to heights she could never reach with me. I am a voyeur; I get thrills watching others perform sex. Watching my wife perform sex on someone else lets me fantasize that she is really with me. Sounds odd, but my thrills come from watching and fantasizing more than being in the midst of it. Secondly, it is a bit masochistic. By watching your partner or wife have sex with another man, you are arousing your jealousy, and that emotion is a wild ride indeed. I do not consider myself an overly jealous person. But my limits would soon be tested.

Studies have been conducted regarding men who imagine their women with other men. The jealousy and competitiveness that is stirred up cause them to reach orgasm more quickly. Maybe I like how my partner teases other men and make them envy the fact that she's all mine. I would put her up on this pedestal, and other guys would crave her. This turned me on big-time.

We had to find a spectacular black stud for Sara the next time we made plans for an evening of fun. I realized that sometimes fantasy should stay fantasy. But, there was the perfect guy out there for us and I would find him. I looked up the word *cuckold* and found this definition:

"Not simply a man whose wife/girlfriend cheats on him, but rather a man who actually gets aroused by knowing or seeing her in sexual situations with other men such as flirting, kissing, fondling, or sex. In particular, situations where he is NOT participating but instead marginalized, just observing, or even completely ignored."

I found more information on cuckolds:

A cuckold husband is someone who finds the idea of his wife having sexual flings with other men highly arousing and stimulating. The cuckold husband attempts to convince his wife to embark on sexual flings with other men, and if successful in this, he will then seek out a man who makes the most desirable partner, in the husband's view, for his wife. In the case of white cuckold husbands, it is almost universal that a bigger, stronger, exceptionally athletic, and possibly younger, black male will be considered as the most acceptable partner for the wife.

This was turning into our situation completely. Once I realized Sara was attracted to black guys, it was a no-brainer.

There are a number of factors that led us in this direction. The black male is seen as physically superior and thus far more capable in terms of sexual activity than the cuckold considers himself to be. My Sara as the younger wife would receive the maximum in terms of sexual stimulation, long-lasting intercourse, and the experience of many exotic positions during intercourse because of the greater strength and endowment of the chosen black stud. There is the *taboo* aspect of it all as well.

Tied into this is the contrast of skin color and the erotic visual it provides when the wife and her sex partner are together. I ended up finding and reading tons of stuff like the above. I came to realize I was by no means alone in my fantasies of such behavior.

Chapter Five

I began searching in earnest for the perfect guy to take my hot wife to sexual heaven. Online I came upon one that fit the bill. A lean, dark-skinned black male who was a trucker happened to travel past our city via interstate every six months. He sent me some pictures of himself in action. Man was he her type! He looked like a pro basketball player—6'4" and all muscle. The action pics he supplied in his email showed his manhood to be long and thick almost beyond imagination. He was what Sara needed and would knock her panties off.

We made plans to meet at a bar the next time he was passing by. Sara was reluctant after our unsatisfactory experience at the Halloween bash prior, yet agreed to meet, hoping for a better arrangement.

When the day arrived, I was a little bit uneasy. I had not heard from Kevin in three days, and he had me wondering what was up. We had picked a place and time earlier in the week but had had no contact since. Sara was kept in the dark about us not talking in three days.

As a backup, I got online and searched for a last-minute replacement. There was no one on the spur of the moment except for a local white guy I came across on instant messenger. He said he'd be thrilled to meet us that evening and gave me his cell number in case things opened up. He looked decent enough, but man was I was hoping Kevin would show up.

Sara dressed up nicely in black slacks and a white blouse. The plan was to have a quick dinner then go below to an adjoining bar at ground level afterwards. I called Kevin several times but received no reply. Sara was disappointed and all dressed up with no one to play with. I told her I knew a white guy I could call; if he was not that great we'd just meet him and not hook up after dinner. She went along with the idea, still downhearted about having no black stud. She had seen Kevin's pics and was ready for a big night. It would have been amazing.

So we waited and met Rick. He seemed nice but sort of preppy. Sara was not all that thrilled. We chatted, ate dinner and headed downstairs, where there was a dance club. Rick was nervous, telling me Sara was lovely. She wanted him to be more flirty and aggressive but he was laid back. He wasn't getting her going. We danced and drank a few purple hooters. At least Sara was having fun. When it came time to consider leaving, she said he was too shy, that she would prefer to leave without him. I knew I had to try and step this game up, so I got him alone in the men's room and told him how to go about a last-ditch effort to get the wife excited. I explained how she wanted to be flirted with, touched and seduced more. He asked what to do, and I said simply, "Tell her she's hot. Dance close to her, rub up against her, kiss her. At the table slide your hand up her leg and play with her inner thigh, tease her, rub her pussy lips. Try hard. If not, we're leaving soon."

I figured it wasn't going to work out, so I settled up our drinks bill. They did, however, dance and I let them also sit alone a while.

Finally I asked her if she was ready and she said yes. So I asked, "Should I tell Rick we're going?" Sara grinned at me. "Yes, I think I want him to join us at a hotel." I'm like, "Huh? I thought you were not interested?" She went on to tell me he had been frisky on the dance floor and she felt turned on now. So off we went. I was really surprised.

In the car she was on fire. As we drove to the cheap hotel she was touching herself already: "Honey, I'm so horny, and I'm wet." All the way to the hotel, stuff like, "Hurry and get there!" It was crazy. She was a different woman suddenly.

Once we got to the hotel, she was on him right away. There was not even time to get my video camera up and running. They frolicked and kissed and stripped down. He slid her red bikini panties down part way revealing her milky thighs. She was actually moaning from the excitement. Soon they were on the bed; she was moaning even more loudly and had him almost naked in no time. He tore her blouse away, sucking her big nipples and ravishing her body.

He pushed her to the bed, sliding her skimpy red string panties to the side. Before he could remove them, she took them off herself. Her bubbly firm butt spilled out, and they embraced passionately, kissing deeply as she whispered, "Please, fuck me good!" in his ear. She pulled his boxers off right away.

He was not that big, which was disappointing. She got on him right away, pushing him to the bed and slipping him into her in one try—no hesitation. She got on top and rode him like a wild lass. Soon she let him get on top, but after the switch he had trouble keeping his erection. It took him time to get it up, but after he did, he came in minutes. She was just getting started and he was done. She tore him up. We would never see him again—that was for sure. He was overwhelmed; his expression said, "Like wow!" As we bolted from the place, she was shaking her head. All I heard in my head was, "I want more, I want it harder, I like it deep, it makes me feel like a woman."

During the week following she was depressed. Rick had not been her type, the drinks had made her reckless, and she felt guilty. It was hard on our marriage. My bride was having regrets. She thought it best to take a break, maybe even giving up swinging all together. Overall, there had been just too many disappointments.

A wife who finds herself married to a cuckold husband will go through a number of emotional phases and behavioral stages. I was seeing that firsthand.

Studies done by several psychologists note that women tend to respond initially to their husband's suggestions and requests and coaxing for sex with another male with shock, dismay, and revulsion. These emotions are soon replaced by genuine worry over whether the husband has lost interest in her sexually, and whether the husband no longer loves her. The cuckold husband will make every effort to calm his wife's fears and worries and get rid of her anger and revulsion by bringing up the subject and doing everything possible to convince her that he not only wants her to take a sex partner, but that he wants her to "expand her sexual horizons" and "experience greater sexual pleasure, stimulation and excitement."

A long time passed before we would try again. We decided to have children. This would have a huge impact on any alternative lifestyle fun. Sara made it a point to say, "Listen—a child will not stop us from doing whatever we decide after the fact." I wondered if this would be the end.

Our child was born, and we were very happy. Another year went by. Sara had finally begun to adjust and get back in shape. It took almost two years before the day would come when the idea of meeting a guy was appealing again. Neither of us considered it until things started to get back to normal.

The time had come; we were ready to try again. We found a local basketball player who was 6'6 and black and planned to meet him at a bar that coming Saturday night. Mikey was as described—tall, lean, athletic and black—and Sara said right off the bat she found him attractive. His head was closely shaven and he had very long arms.

So this time, we were off to a good start. Sara looked great that evening. Her long, curly blond hair cascaded about her angel face, and her sexy, well-rounded body was packed nicely into her jean skirt and tight blouse. We made time with tall Mikey, and the two seemed like they were getting along. He, however, seemed somewhat shy; I had no idea where things would lead. He was not a big dancer, so we mostly talked.

The night was going by pretty fast, and it was getting late. We hit a few bars together and in the end it was time to head to our hotel. Mikey said he'd join us in a while, so it was just the two of us when we left the bar. When we arrived at our hotel room, Sara said she liked Mikey and was excited to party with him. After about twenty minutes he called my cellphone to say he was outside. I went out to greet him.

When we met outside the door, I was frank with him. "Mikey, I have to tell you something. Sara is excited about playing with you. Don't chat much. Join her on the bed, touch her and be playful. She wants to get naked, but it's getting late and she's not a night owl." Basically I was telling her to go for it right off. The hour was late, and she'd be tired very soon. He agreed, and up we went to our suite.

We talked for over an hour. It was nearing two in the morning. I was frustrated and impatient to make things happen. I said, "Guys, it's getting really late. I mean, are you two going to play some, or should we call it a night?" That statement finally got them going. Sara was all for playing, and Mikey and she got close.

Lying on the bed, they embraced, kissed, and started to undress each other. He was very dark and tall and she, very white and small. His hands were all over her curves. She was hot and ready. As they fondled each other, I saw his cock for the first time. It was only average size in soft form. When she finally stroked it, it grew in thickness and size until it was maybe eight inches. They spooned on the bed, kissing and nibbling. He slid his fingers in her now moist love canal.

She urged him to fuck her. He put on a condom and they were soon locked in missionary. She moaned with joy, and he pushed in with one try. Outside the room I had made it a point to tell him that I wanted to see her on top, riding him, so he changed into cowgirl position; she got on and was bouncing hard. He only did it a minute before turning her over doggy. He got aggressive then and starting pounding into her. I heard her start to moan louder and look uncomfortable. She called out, "Easy now," as he pounded harder and harder. He then grunted, "Oh yeah, arrrrrrh." It was too fast. He was coming already. Sara was disappointed and masturbated in front of us. It was really late when we parted ways.

Sara offered me a quick mercy fuck and I came in two minutes. Since he had come inside her—even though he'd worn a condom—we were nervous for weeks afterward. This fear of pregnancy was going to place a huge damper on our lives. A looming guilt bothered us both. I hated it so much. Sara loved sex. Sara loved to fuck. Sara hated guilt; it overwhelmed her in every way.

Several months passed. We needed to meet a black guy who was bigger and would last longer and really give Sara the fuck of her life. The next week I found such a guy on an online swingers' site; his personal caught my eye. One comment on his profile was enough for me to go ahead and make arrangements to meet. We would have to take a long four-hour ride, but I thought it would be worth it. The comment said, "This guy has the largest cock I HAVE EVER SEEN."

We set the date and time to meet. Just the thought was turning me on. Sara agreed it would be fun, so things were looking up for our swinging lifestyle. Ken, however, was older, and that was the one thing that bothered me about this meeting. I knew Sara liked them younger. But he looked good and was so huge that I put aside my concerns over his age as the meet came closer. Our sex life was not all that good. For one thing, with our new son in the mix, we never had time. With different schedules and what not, we made love hardly at all. Sara was not all that romantic a woman, and unless I planned something special with a sitter or went out of my way to initiate, we never fucked. I could only jerk off looking at her pictures and videos. I just found it too difficult. The buildup and the letdown were not appealing to me. I wanted her to have a great lay, not little old me.

I wondered what a cuckold should actually look like. Was I typical, or a rare breed? I was not a wimp when it came to physical form. I worked out, looked decent enough, and certainly was a friendly guy. I guess I was a little older and my wife was a hot babe, but was that what a cuckold truly was? In life we come in all shapes and sizes. In this context I supposed that was true as well.

The weekend for our meet with the monster cock black guy arrived. He was named Ken, and I recalled us meeting another Ken way back. We drove the long distance to a nearby state. We met him at the designated bar, where he was already sipping a cocktail. He was older than his picture, and Sara was taken aback. I thought, "Oh shit; what a long drive to take for this!" He was decent-looking in an older sort of way. He had an officer's haircut, was slim and carried himself nicely. We sat together and had a bite to eat. He was personable and a navy officer in the service, just back from Germany. He was excited to meet such a young sexy lass as my wife. His eyes looked her up and down. I was hoping she'd come around.

She seemed reluctant to get too friendly. After I got her a few glasses of wine, things got a little more relaxed. She wore a skirt that night; I made a point of slipping my hand up her skirt while sitting next to them in the bar corner. I played with her pussy constantly for the hour we chatted, getting her very wet. She didn't resist the idea of some hotel room fun when we decided to take the chatting up to our suite. In the room they embraced, and he lay her down on the bed, fingering her for quite some time. She was lost in hotness. He massaged her large breasts and kissed her deeply. Sara was getting into it, and I got my video camera going.

Finally, after a lot of heavy petting, he pulled off of her. She was excited and he was hard. I could see the huge bulge in his shorts, and I was like, *holy molly what a giant head on that dong*. I truly had never seen a bulge that big in my life. He sat back to remove his shorts, and when I first saw his specimen I was in shock. He had the largest, thickest, most magnificent penis I had ever laid eyes on. He was so big it was surreal.

Sara unhooked her bra, which left her in nothing but tiny panties. She pressed on him and reached back to grasp his cock. I knew she was surprised that she had to use both hands to get a firm stroke on it. She had a hard time wrapping her tiny hand over that thing. I was taping the encounter with a video recorder and in looking back my own voice is heard saying, "holy shit" right on the microphone.

They tussled on the hotel bed. He was as hard as a rock—firm and ready. He looked to the nightstand and grabbed an extra-large magnum condom. Sara slid off him and to the side, slipping out of her frilly thong panties. I caught her glance over at him and at his tool, then directly at me with an astounded expression. Her eyes were jumping out of her head and they said, *holy crap what have I gotten into here?*

He couldn't even get the extra large magnum condom on in a normal slide-over fashion. Guys always slide a condom on, it's that simple. Today one can get large-sized condoms, even extra large. But this guy would not be able to just slip on a condom of any size. He had to stretch it like a wide balloon to place it over his black dick. He got it on and proceeded to get on top of my wife. His dark black skin was glistening now from pre-sweat as he pressed into her pale white form. His dong was still standing hard and he positioned it near Sara's opening. Her pussy had been fingered for quite awhile and she was wet and her lips, which are pronounced, were protruding and swelled out.

Usually Sara takes a swinger partner easily and without reservations. No extra lubrication is ever needed. The penis enters in one try. This was not the case this time. Sara slid her hand on his shaft and tried to ease him in her wetness. He eased in slowly, but still she kept holding his fat prick, trying to guide him. I had never seen this happen before. She was also sliding back as he pressed in. Her body moved toward the headboard and he tried to get in deeper. She continued to help his shaft guide in, and it wasn't until her head hit the headboard that there was no stopping the penetration. She finally let go of his cock and went in deeper. She moaned very loudly.

    He was not at all rough as he slowly began to push in and out of her. She cried out, "Holy God, you are so big!" "Holy Jesus, you're big, sooooooo big." He pushed deeper and began to get a rhythm. She was easing into his giant manhood and soon found her own movements working with his. Her legs began to bounce up and down and she groaned and squealed in passion. "You are sooooo Huge," she cried out.

    "Wow, oh God, you're sooooooo huge." Sara grabbed his ass then and they fucked steadily. She took him all very deep and his cock was wet and glistening as it went in and out of her. She was lost in the deepest, most serious fuck of her life.

    What a change it was from my tiny, thin four inches. They pounded together for a while, and he put her on her side to ease his weight off. We could never do this posture; I am not big enough, and her bubbly ass would deflect any change of me pushing in. He did so easily, and they fucked again for a while. His massive tool glistened, sliding in and out; she took it freely and with ease, lying on her side. I was lost in the view, amazed at what was happening. She encouraged his orgasm and he got back on her—fully on top, pressing firmly on her small frame. I wanted her to ride him—it would be incredible—but that did not happen. He pumped hard to an explosion of his juices. *Oh God; I had forgotten to tell him to pull out—and so had Sara.* He had a condom on, but what if it broke or had a hole? I was sacred as hell. It seemed the condom held as he was out, and I saw no leaks. Sara was still hot. She masturbated right then and there in front of us and came loudly.

We would worry for weeks over whether the condom might have had a small hole in it. She was on the pill, but what if that failed?

Our guy left the hotel rather quickly after Sara said she was very tired. There was silence in the room and I knew she was upset. I was crazy horny and took her for a quick one-minute screw. I came fast. I was thinking this guy could be our regular meet once per month; perhaps we could meet just him and no other? For the first time the law of the Kama Sutra genitalia size chart was a match in our marriage and in Sara's vaginal size opening.

But it was not to be. She was feeling guilty and very upset all of a sudden. Crying, she told me she had not wanted to fuck him. She had done it because he had traveled a long ways to meet. He had been too old for her; the attraction had not really been there. She got lost in the liquid courage of the drinks and then the wanting for sex but now she felt awful. I was sad, too. I had thought we had hit the jackpot. As we went to sleep in the hotel room, I was still overexcited. I played with myself constantly all through the night and kept waking her to fuck. She thought I had lost my mind.

Half awake and in a dream state, I envisioned him—this older monster-sized dong military man—as her full time lover. He would be our main squeeze. He and Sara would form a monthly joining, with me as the helpful cuckold. I was not bi—never once had I seen myself as such—but with him I would do my duty. I would suck his giant prick to get him hard; I would eat her cream pie when he was done with her each night. I would be the ass fucker when a double penetration was called for. I would serve drinks and do anything they needed to make each night special. These thoughts had never crossed my mind before.

In the morning I came to realize it would be the end of our swinging days for quite a while. By waking her up several times to fuck her and saying that just maybe she could reconsider and meet him once per month, I had only made matters worse. She declared an end to all our swinging on the long ride home. She quit the lifestyle. Never had she felt more upset. She had made up her mind never to bed anyone unless she was very attracted to them. The aftereffects drained her soul. This time was no exception, and we were done with our open marriage.

The following weekend, therefore, was apparently a fluke. Sara and I were out dancing at a club. She wore designer jeans and a tight black blouse; she looked fantastic. Her long blond curly locks whipped about on the dance floor and her bubble butt packed tight in those hot jeans was a showstopper. The luck of the night gave us two fairly good-looking stylish black men that were buddies. Both eyed Sara intently.

They made it a point to smile at us and eventually came over to make small talk. One even asked Sara to dance. The night was getting wild and wilder by the minute. These guys seemed cool and mentioned that a few friends were having a party nearby; they would love it if we attended. They were ready to go, and we had a big decision to make. After sipping her purple hooters, Sara was all for it.

The party was held at a rural home on the east side. The place was older, and when we first entered, somewhat dimly lit. Three more black guys were playing cards at a table, and a few hot-looking Latino ladies were sitting nearby on a low, king-sized bed. The main area was a gutted-out playroom. Introductions were made and we ended up joining the card game. The drinks flowed freely. A few guys were smoking cigars and the room got hazy and we were laughing and having a crazy fun time. I lost one hundred dollars too quick, and my wallet was running dry.

Sara giggled and wanted to play more. The men were eying her closely and I saw one lick his lips. Two of the guys were twins; I mean they must have been identical. They had on wife-beater white tank tops, and their short dread-top hairstyles matched, too. Everyone encouraged us to keep playing, to keep betting. I was like thinking *we have no money*, but they vouched for us, saying, "If you don't have the cash, we'll figure something out." This was kind of nuts, but I was sort of drunk, and my wife was into it, determined to beat these guys at poker. I sucked at poker because I hardly ever played, but I went along with the game.

We lost again. Suddenly the men all got up and demanded Sara as their reward. I was like, "Are you guys nuts?" She resisted and felt the same. We were ready to leave. The two girls sitting nearby left the room. The guys grabbed Sara and pulled her over to the low-standing bed. I tried to cut them off, but one shoved me back. They stripped Sara's clothes off—yanking her jeans down, leaving her white and pink polka dotted bikini panties half on one ass cheek and one leg. They tossed her onto the bed, pulling her jeans fully off. The panties followed. I cried out, "Guys, this is nuts! Let her go." She fought them, but there was too many. A heavily tattooed one called Brand got her top over her head, and he all but pulled her bra free—brutally, with no regard for her.

The men gathered around my wife were removing their own clothes next. *What the fuck was happening here? This was friggin crazy!* The twins brandished cocks that were unworldly; they looked like long thick vodka bottles, each with slimming tips, uncircumcised heads covered with foreskin. The others, too, were hung and hard. They all pounced on my little wife. I was dizzy, yet ready to do anything I could to stop the onslaught. "Stop this you fucking assholes!" I yelled as I dove in to break it all up. I grabbed one of the guys and was about to punch his face in, but another drove me back with a shoulder block. I tumbled to a corner of the room. I got back up and shouted more, furious. Sara was begging to be let loose; she was upset and drunk.

The thugs were in-between her legs, eating her pussy. Others stuck their cocks in her face, while another sucked her nipples. I went forward again, mad as hell. I took two steps and found myself staring in the face of a snub-nosed revolver. Jebron, the tallest of the black brutes, looked at me with a big grin. "Sit down over there and shut your fucking mouth, white boy." I backed into a small chair and sat and watched. The men ravished my wife. The room was spinning and they laughed and chuckled and used her body. One now fucked her doggie style. Another had her sucking his long erection. Another sucked her tits. She had resisted at first, but it looked like now she had given in to the sex. One of the twins got under her and jutted his huge tube-steak black dong up into her pussy. From behind, one licked her ass and anally entered her. She was taking a double penetration. She was wildly not ready for this. She wanted to be let go. The others held onto her, one stuffing his prick in her yelping mouth. They told her to shut up and take it.

The gangster with all the tats grabbed his box nearby and demanded that all the brothers stop, as he trying to accomplish something. The men held her in place as he inked her ass. He wove a black spade on her butt, giving my delicate wife a permanent tattoo. I was in shock. He added, "bbc whore" for his name, and this symbol of a black spade representing her as a black-cock-loving slut was now hers forever. I was sweating buckets, shaking and breathless. Suddenly all the men were joyously ejaculating, coming all over my wife, spurting their jism on her face, ass, swollen pussy lips and even her hair. This wetness awoke me from my slumber. "Holy fucking shit," I murmured.

I had been dreaming.

I staggered into the hallway, leaving Sara in our bed. I leaned against the wall, wiping sweat and heat off my soaked face and neck. What a wild-ass dream. I ran my hand over my forehead, squeezing and shaking, to gain a grip on myself. This had been one of the most vivid dreams I had ever experienced.

I thanked God that it had only been a dream. I could not get back to sleep. I was able to include the dream in this book in such detail because I recorded it in my journals. It was an easy one to remember, and to be honest most dreams I have had in my life were forgotten by the next morning. I would not forget this one anytime soon. In truth, this book is a compilation of all my journal writings.

Another year went by, and I missed the rush of swinging and the visual of sex. No more crazy dreams either. As a voyeur I needed to see some action soon. I had met another couple online who wanted the wife to meet some black men and decided to help them out. I set up a party for the guy's wife at a hotel out of state. I would be host for the event. Several men had approached me about wanting to meet my wife, but she had quit the lifestyle. I thought, *here are all these men, why not give another guy's wife her fantasy night come true?* Sara agreed to let me do it, and I made arrangements for the bash to take place in a few weeks.

In a typical marriage, a wife is usually younger than her hubby or the same age. This was the case for us. As a result, a woman's increasing sexual appetite in her 30s and 40s gives her greater sexual needs than her husband's. This was true for us as well. The wife needs more sex, and longer sessions, and more orgasms than her spouse. Her older-or-same-age husband, on the other hand, wants sex far less than his wife. This can of course leave his wife unsatisfied and frustrated.

Finally, the thing that makes most sense in regard to a woman's sexual superiority is her ability to have multiple orgasms. There is a big difference. It's just that darn emotional factor that tends to mess it all up when trying to live a cuckold lifestyle. Women have been raised and programmed to think that too much sex or sex with many men is wrong. The guilt kills them, and for my Sara guilt was a very big issue through our many encounters.

By allowing Sara to engage in sex with other men I was relieved of the pressure to perform. So-called normal couples and people in general would find this off-kilter, to say the least. But there is no cheating in a cuckold marriage, no lies, and no boredom. This was a great setup, or so I thought.

I, in the meantime, had begun to try to find ways to make our own sex life better. Sara and I just could not find common ground as a couple in the fucking department. I bought sex toys to enhance the activity, but none seemed to get her going. I got anal beads, jelly dildos, vibrators, and all sorts of lotions and lingerie for her to mess around with. We found no common ground with any of these add-ons. I picked up strap-on cocks, offered to do anything she wanted—weird stuff as well—but again nothing. She wanted just plain sex, yet she wanted it to last for hours, with a really hard cock driving deep and steady. She wanted me to whisper sweet nothings and make it all just perfect, yet this was not working either.

So I put my energy into the party with another two couples whose wives loved sexy black men. I scheduled two wives and eight black men for a Saturday-night party to be held in two weeks. When the evening arrived, I tried to interest Sara in going, but she said no thanks. So off I went on the three-hour drive to a nice hotel in Boston. I met first with a couple who lived about an hour from the hotel. She was a sexy, forty-something woman with short curly hair and a nice attitude. She wore a black miniskirt and black fishnet stockings. Her blouse was a silky white, and she looked real good. Her husband was a solid guy yet seemed to have an attitude I did not click with. He was the wealthy-husband type with an oversexed wife who he let run free, yet he wanted full control of the situation because he had a high-profile job. He was stiff, so I was glad that she at least was fun and had personality. While he got drinks, we talked, and she was thrilled with the setup for the evening. She told me, "I am so excited about this night. I work hard and love sex and want to play all night. I deserve it and need this type of fun whenever possible."

We waited at a bar right next to the hotel for the rest of the guests to show up. The first black guy to arrive was a real charmer. He was dressed nice, good looking, had a clean-shaven head, was fit and had a huge grin at all times on his face. He hugged Mary (the wife of Curt) and she was all smiles. He romanced her at the bar table and had her happy and into the foreplay as soon as they began chatting. This was his game and he was on it quickly. She told me I had made a great choose for Guy One.

The second guy to arrive was not so great. He was short and had a mouth on him that did not fit his size, yet he was nice enough to fit in. We waited for the next guy and the other couple, who were all expected to join us. None did, however, so we all headed to the hotel room to begin the fun. I was just supposed to be the host and enjoy watching. I got a call saying the second couple was canceling. This did not sit well with Curt, whose wife would now be the sole object of desire for all the men. A third black guy showed up, and we ended up having Mary enjoy all three while Curt and I watched. This new guy was a stocky fellow with a decent smile and all three wasted no time taking Mary to excited heights in the living room area. She was on fire, ready and willing.

While we had walked to the hotel, the charismatic Tyron had been making her steamy, touching her and teasing her with foreplay. Upon arriving in the room, he slipped off her micro miniskirt and offered up her pussy for all to see. The shorter fellow named Al was loving it and fondling her small tits. Eric the third guy picked her up, and they all carried her to the bed. I peered in, watching the men strip her naked and go to town. She was passionate and loved every second of it. She had no trouble with all six sets of hands all over her petite frame. Each guy would have her that evening. Tyron made sure he was first; he got naked and brandished a big, thick, mushroom-umbrella-headed cock that she sucked furiously and made long and hard. I thought to myself, *wow, this guy would be perfect for my Sara*. They fucked in all postures and the two other black guys even did a double penetration on Mary.

In the living room area of the suite, Tyron and I had a chance to talk. He was a big sports fan like myself and very funny. I made sure to mention my wife to him and he was interested. The night ended with all of us talking and sharing stories and whatnots. I had no desire to ever see the other black guys again. They were in no way my sexy wife's types. But, man this Tyron fit the bill. We exchanged e-mails.

Mary said she had a wonderful night, very hot. Her husband thanked me for playing host, yet he was still stiff. We watched a little of the baseball game on TV before heading our separate ways. During my long drive home I called Sara to say I wished she had made the trip. She was asleep and our conversation went nowhere.

The next week Sara and I didn't discuss swinging. But when Friday night came and we found ourselves with time to talk, things exploded. She had decided swinging was not for her, and I decided it was the one thing that made our sex life prosper. Our argument was heated. She loved the idea of great sex but had been raised Catholic and felt it was wrong. Every time we met someone, we got all excited and had sex more often. It felt right to me. We discussed the idea of one lover for her. We could arrange for one special black lover, who would fuck her regularly on a monthly basis. That interested her, yet we came to no agreement. I mentioned Tyron from the party I'd hosted and explained how good-looking he was and funny and all the things she loved in a sexy guy. That, too, held her interest, but we made no plans to resume any swinging activity.

Time passed and we tried hard to make things work in the sex department. Our size difference, my impotence and our work schedules with a child made it very difficult. In my spare time I came to realize a lot of husbands were into this cuckold stuff. There were so many websites about the subject, with tons of ads seeking men for their wives. More parties caught my attention too. There were black and white parties with an interracial theme. One party had all the cuckolds stay on one side of the room, while wives went to the other, closed off by a wall. The black men on that side would meet the women separately and chitchat. Once the bar pickup strategy was over, husbands were allowed to join in. By then the ladies had made their choice or choices for the evening. One even had the wives wearing a white T-shirt so that all the black men could use a sharpie and comment on said wife so that hubbies could read the notes.

Why in the world did all these guys—not unlike myself—love seeing their wives get fucked and seduced by other men? There was a hotwife and cuckold phenomenon going on and most of the so-called normal adults had no clue. Sara worked with the most stuck-up, plain, reserved people in the world. There was no chance that she would gain insight or get excited about exploring her sexuality at work. I got lost in my fantasies for a while. I'd play with myself to her sexy pics, and the few videos with her as the star became my outlet.

Chapter Six

As the months flew by, I mentioned Tyron a lot. Eventually she said, "What the hell; let's go for it, he seems like someone I'd like to meet." I knew she would find him cool. It was a winning solution to our current stalemate. I hoped they would hit it off and she could find some newfound excitement in swinging.

I showed Tyron a few pics of Sara on an email and he was quite taken by her looks. So it looked like we had a date. We made plans to meet him at a bar halfway between our homes.

That evening Sara decided to dress casual. She had a pair of Capri pants that were a camel color and fit real tight to her shapely ass. These pants gave her a pumpkin most women would die for. She put on a tight V-neck brown shirt and completed the outfit with a pair of sexy brown and gold heels. Her long blond hair cascaded down her shoulders, curly and shiny. The bar we had chosen was two stories; one was outside—below and on the street itself—and the other part was upstairs, inside the adjoining building.

As live bands blasted music about the streets, we waited outside for Tyron to arrive. The cocktail of the night was a mocha martini. Sara loved this drink, and before the night was over would two more. One thing is for sure: whenever she drinks she gets super horny and her inhibitions go out the door. It's what I call her liquid courage.

Tyron our sexy black date arrived on time and sat between us. He was dressed in slacks and a long-sleeved button-down shirt, very dressy and sharp. He poured on the charm right away. He kissed her and smiled and reached for her drink, saying, "This looks interesting."

Tyron was bald and slim and fairly tall. He had decent muscles and a great smile. The two of them chatted and he whispered in her ear something that made her giggle. He then talked about the people around us, insisting that each one had a hidden agenda for the evening. Sara laughed and got into their conversation. More drinks arrived and the two got lost in talking as I watched and listened to the loud band nearby. I could not make out what he was saying but he kept flirting with her for an hour and she was into it. I was left out of the loop. I sat there like a good husband, saying nothing.

Finally I suggested that we should head upstairs to the dance club. I had a hard time getting their attention for God's sake. We made our way up and Sara took the lead.

Tyron saw her standing for the first time. His eyes darted all over her ass, and he was grinning from ear to ear while looking back at me. Her ass was sticking straight out in her tight camel capris and the heels complemented her calves. The blond curly locks twirled about her back, running down to her waist, and he couldn't help but notice her full 34c bosom uplifted by her brown Victoria Secret underwired bra below her V-neck shirt.

He loved what he saw. We got new drinks and hit the dance floor for a few songs. After the first two songs, I made it a point to leave them alone to dance, and they seemed to get along well. Afterward we got a table and chatted for some time. Sara was getting drunk, and I tried to monitor her drinking. But she was lost in the night. Cutting her off was not easy.

Giddy as hell, she told us casually, "Well … here I am with two men. I don't know who to go home with." Those words shocked me. There would be no more martinis, yet she kept demanding them. I finally got her to calm down. I asked if she wanted all three of us to head back to the nearby hotel. She said, "Okay, that could be fun," so we made our way back through the big crowd downstairs and outside into the streets. She yelled out, "I say we head to the beach and enjoy the ocean right now." I was like, huh? It was midnight.

As Tyron followed us back to the hotel, Sara and I got into a heated argument. I had brought along a small DVD camera to record any sexual play. She said outright, "I do not want you to use that recorder." I was upset, having planned to use the footage to jerk off to in the future. I knew these two would match up well in the bedroom. She was going on about not wanting to be on tape and all.

A little upset and bummed over all her comments and the intimacy of her and this Black stud's conversations, I said, "Why don't we just skip this and tell him to head home." That prompted her to rethink her demands. She was like, "Well I guess the taping is okay." I looked at her and said, "Are you sure?" She was like, "Yes. I'm so horny and he is so hot, I want him, plain and simple." So that was it. We went over to his car and invited him up to our room.

Tyron was not a newbie. He carried a bag of goodies with him, like a gigolo in heat. It contained an iPod, speakers, drinks, mints, magnum extra-large condoms, and all sorts of weird stuff. Sara was still giddy and went right for his drinks. He put on some music—hip-hop type songs, mostly by black rap singers. These songs were all about fucking, pussy, and partying to the limit. The music added to the mood, and they took little time embracing on the bed. He slowly worked his magic.

I got the DVD camera going and, for what seemed like an eternity, the two of them kissed, cuddled, and chatted on the bed. This was nuts. *Get to the fucking please,* I thought. But no nudity was coming any time soon. They were slowly petting, easing into almost two hours of foreplay. I shut the camera down twice, tired of holding it. This nearly two hours of touching and whispering-sweet-nothings was too much. Tyron finally undid Sara's pants, and I grabbed the camera once again. She was passionate and aflame with desire. I knew what he had packing and how she would be sent into orbit by his technique and size. Her top and bra came off, revealing her tits. There would be an hour of touching and teasing next. There was my wife, Sara down to only her teeny pink frilly top panties, enjoying every minute of it. I watched, loving that her nails and toenails were a matching shiny pink color.

Tyron was in no rush to explore her body. Soon after sliding off her panties, he had his shirt off, too. Thinking the action would now heat up, I was excited to see it go down, yet tired of the wait. My own member was aching now. I was aroused and semi-hard. He licked at her body for a while and dove into her sweet cunt for at least thirty minutes. She was glowing with want, but he was not ready to stop or get undressed. But Sara had had enough finally, and she reached to undo his trousers. After he helped her take off his slacks, she immediately reached for his cock. They rolled on the bed, embracing and kissing passionately. Sara was now pushing at his swollen jockey-short hidden penis with her foot, neatly fondling it. She then used her hands to peel the shorts back. Excitedly she revealed his big, thick, mushroomed-headed prick. Her eyes glazed over and she was lost in the moment. His dong was long and thick, the centerpiece a giant umbrella-shaped head. Sara was in for it tonight.

Tyron was not rushing, even at this time. They kissed fervently, over and over. I was getting bored; there was no hardcore action. I wanted her to fuck. I wanted her to feel a real man inside her. This is what I was waiting for—sex and lots of sex. This kissing and sweet whispering were driving me nuts. But he waited and waited, kissing her neck and flirting. Then she went for his cock, stroking its big head and leaning in for a blowjob. He was a lucky man. Sara never sucked me or any other guy unless there was a big attraction. She sucked him a while, slowly swallowing his meat. He got harder and more swollen; she was on fire. His big head swelled her tiny moth. It was an amazing sight. Finally he slid on top of her, and the first penetration occurred. She grabbed his ass and pulled him in deeper and deeper. They molded together in unison.

HE FUCKED HER. She loved it, pumping back hard into him. Music fed their emotions. "Party like a Rock Star" was the initial push–in-and-pump-her tune that played in the room. They would screw for at least an hour. She was so wet, so open, so inviting. They kissed and fucked then kissed some more. The sex was never ending. I wondered about so much kissing. Perhaps I should not have allowed it. She was giddy and for the first time unaware of me in the room or of my existence. Too much affection was going on. She told him, "I love your cock, and you feel so good, so right, so deep." I was asked to get them some water. Then, to get them a towel, to change the music and do whatever they asked.

When they finally had finished a long session of pumping, they again held each other tight. More whispering, more sweet talk, more kisses. It was nearing three in the morning, and there I sat. My head was spinning. "I want more, I want it harder, I like it deep, it makes me feel like a woman."

He slid her into the spoon position next. Himself, behind her, guiding his long erection into her wanting love hole. This made for a perfect posture, and she quickly manipulated her clitoris as he pushed in and out of her. She was very titillated now, and he used her with a bump and grind technique that only spurred on her own. Being able to touch her love button while still fucking was a new thrill to her. They humped for twenty minutes. Hip-hop music spurred them on, and she was flush with satisfaction. Her I'm-going-to-get-off glow was appearing, and she began to yelp more and more as he pushed in and out. Her hand flicked harder and harder on her love button and she groaned louder and louder: "Ohhhh yeess, I'm coming, yessss, oh baby, baby, oooooooooh." Sara collapsed on the bed, rolling onto her belly. That ass, that killer bubble butt, stuck right up, however, and Tyron had to slap it. She tumbled about with him. Sara got on top and kissed him wildly. I now fully saw her gash. Those pouty lips were so big, so open. It was incredible. I wanted her to ride his fat dick. But they fell to the side and cuddled.

It was nearly three-thirty in the morning and Sara was not a night person. However, she was excited again and stroked his hard cock to erection and pulled him onto her for more. She moaned loudly. They fucked again, kissing and melding into one another. She was wet all over her ass and swollen pussy lips. I watched her take his thick black cock easily, deep inside her hungry vagina. His fat mushroom tip pushed her soft cunt lips smoothly open.

More fucking followed, an even longer session than before. I thought it would never end. She urged him on: "Yes, that's it; do me, fuck me, give it to me, harder, harder, oh yes, make me scream."

He exploded for the first time; I mean, he had held off all night. The event was over. They embraced and did not want to part. I literally had to push him out the door and take back my wife for myself. I slipped into her with one push and came right away. She was half awake and could care less. She fell asleep, and in the morning was still turned on. On the drive back, she even masturbated in the car—a first in our swinging lifetime. She looked at me for approval and stated the following: "Wow, that was awesome. What a fun time honey."

Little did I know this would be a huge turning point in our alternative lifestyle.

The following week Sara was still turned on by the encounter. She suddenly loved swinging and was hot for more fun. That Wednesday she had lunch with an old friend who we had first met in the lifestyle. The woman Lainy was a full-fledged swinger who loved the concept and freedom of regularly enjoying new mates. Sara was nuts over Tyron and told her friend she wanted to meet him a lot.

Their conversation that weekend made it back to me, and we sat and talked for a while about where to go at this point. Sara mentioned how Lainy felt swinging was great and that Sara should assure me there was to be no jealousy; she'd never leave me for a black lover. Sara mentioned that the sex had been amazing and so perfect. She slipped and told me I was no comparison. I was a little taken back, but nonetheless turned on that we could swing again. I would make it a point not to meet Tyron anytime soon, but to take advantage of this new excitement and meet other new people.

Yet we would meet Tyron again in due course of time. To tide Sara over I printed a few erotic shots of the two I had taken that night and slipped them in her drawer near our bed. I also purchased a large, vibrating, realistic black rubber dildo for the drawer. I had a plan to see if Sara found the pics and dildo to her liking. I placed the dildo in a certain place to test whether it had been moved at all. I also turned the pictures in a certain way and order to determine if they, too, had been viewed.

Each day I would observe the placement of the toy and pics of Sara and Tyron. I was surprised to find that almost daily the dong and pics had been adjusted and moved about. She was using them to masturbate regularly. I was taken aback. I asked her a few times if she liked them, and she said she did, that they were a turn-on and the toy was good. But I also asked if she was playing with herself to them a lot and she denied it. She did say that every once in awhile she would.

As the weeks passed, I observed the placement of these objects almost every day. They had always been moved. The dildo changed sides or ends, and the pics were in a new order. Sara was getting off a lot more then she admitted. I had to run with it though. She envisioned many sessions with Tyron in the future and began to eat healthy, exercise constantly, and buy extra sexy clothing and shoes. She was in heat, trying to lure her new mate in, getting off each night thinking about what was to come. I found myself excited yet cautious. *I should have not allowed the kissing,* I kept telling myself. It led to a lot of feelings and deeper bonding.

Our sex was limited and never close to what she experienced with her lover, so we fucked infrequently. I began planning a new encounter, having found a guy another couple claimed was great. I had to find only topnotch guys for Sara. The guy was to meet us at a strip club a few hours from our place, and we made plans the coming weekend to hook up. He was younger. That was a good thing, as she likes young. She demanded more sex from me that month. I did my best but I could sense her dissatisfaction.

The meet-up weekend had come. The strip club was bouncing and the girls were dancing up a storm. We sipped drinks while waiting for Alan to arrive. Sara was excited because her last encounter had been the best ever. If this new guy came close to Tyron she would have a wonderful night indeed. When he arrived he looked good to me, but Sara stated he seemed shy and was just okay. We watched some dancers and I suggested we head right to the hotel. If the scene at the club was not going to be exciting, why wait? Sara needed that teasing warm-up, and it was obvious this fellow was not going to fit the bill.

We exited and headed to a Motel 6 nearby—nothing special, a room, a bed, a sexy blonde and a black guy. Oh I almost forgot ... a husband with a camera as well. Sara was still on fire from the Tyron meet, so she went ahead with our modest private party.

I played our iPod, popping out the latest hip-hop tunes, and they got comfy. Soon they danced a bit and undressed each other. Sara was semi into it but seemed to be having a good time. As he undressed her he had no build up game; he went right for her pussy and licked away. Sara loves the slow get-her-all-excited style, but Alan wanted her quick. He sucked her clit and went to town. Sara looked right up at me and whispered, "I want Tyron." Reading her lips I could only frown.

One thing was going down that I knew would work well. While licking her, Alan had slipped his pants off, and he was thick and huge in the dick department, in fact very big. The fit would be there. My wife would get her hardcore fuck.

She was ready when he put it in her. She yelped for joy. They went at it like two wild beasts. The fit worked—she wide open and wanting, he thick, swollen and huge. When she finally got on top after he and she were in missionary, the real pounding commenced. Sara rode his big prick like a woman in heat, bouncing hard up and down on nice fat inches of black meat. She fucked for an hour, just straddling his dong. She was wet and loved it. The music blasted the tune, "Come on baby take a ride with me." It was a perfect song for my honey bunny to bounce to. They went on to fuck another hour in various positions. She got her sex on like no other could. I had a wife who was so wet, so wide, yet so small in stature, I could only shake my head in amazement. If people had known how much she could take—how much of a pounding by such a big cock—they, too, would shake their heads in utter bewilderment.

During the drive home all I heard was Tyron this and Tyron that. I had to make a serious move for our next meet or she would end up demanding we meet him alone from then on. As I thought about our lifestyle and that Tyron meet, I recalled his thoughts on the encounter. "Sara is great," he had said. "She is surely in my top ten." These words lingered in my head as we drove home, Sara fast asleep beside me. "She has a great ass, just like I love, gorgeous hair, and is the fun type, with personality." I chuckled as I fought to stay awake on the long dark highway home.

I began a serious attempt to find the hottest, most well-spoken sexy black guys on the net. I searched swinger sites far and wide, even looking in far-away states. I could only hope to find a guy who would take Sara's mind off her lover and onto the new stud. I located a guy couples were posting rave reviews about. The reviews on his profile said he was super cool, ten inches, long lasting, fun, sexy and hot. He was also young and looked real good and in great shape. But he lived quite a long distance from us. Luck would have it that he traveled and would be willing to meet nearby. If we could travel a few states over we could all hook up. I showed Sara his pics, and she and Rod spoke on the phone.

We set it up. Rod had teased her on the phone, and this got her excited. My girl loved the charismatic type.

In the meantime things were interesting at home. The sex was limited. I could feel her dissatisfaction in our love play. I, too, found myself desiring to see her well-cocked, deep-dicked to utter pleasure. I got a few comments about my beard and my pubic hair again. She hinted that her lover Tyron had been clean-shaven and that his pubic region had also been shaven bare. She longed for the hours of foreplay and the hard fucking whenever her aching wet pussy craved it. I could not stay hard that long nor be at her cunt's beck and call for hours. I would masturbate a lot while viewing her pics and any video footage of her. My small, shriveled penis could not get hard easily these days unless I saw her in action, in the nude, her pussy open and taking big fat black licorice sticks.

There came a point now when I had to make sure Sara would wear her wedding band and diamond at each meet up. She always kept her band on, but in certain situations she did not wear the matching diamond. I felt they both were a must while bedding these men. I find it funny that when a man wears his wedding ring, women pretty much want nothing to do with said male. On the other hand a woman's wedding band makes little difference to men. Sometimes it even encourages their pursuit.

In the meantime we developed a party-song list. A playlist of songs Sara liked to fuck to, so to speak. For cuckold couples I will list some of the most played songs: "Wipe Me Down," "Milkshake," "Party Like a Rock Star," "Me So Horny," "My Humps," "I want to fuck you like an Animal," "Creame," "Booty Meat," "Low," "Gold Digger," "Feel Like Fuckin," "Walk it Out," "Get Busy," and "White Girl."

We met Rod at a bar the following weekend. He was handsome in an exotic way and Sara seemed pleased. We sat and chatted at a table while they giggled and flirted. He had dreadlocks that she found sexy. He commented that she was hot and guided her hand under the table onto his hard cock. She was titillated, and we left the bar early. Our hotel room was nearby and we arrived ready for some fun. Sara was playful and danced to a hip-shaking Shakira song called "Hips don't Lie," for Rod, getting him all excited. She shook her bubble butt and teased him to the music; he revealed his long ten-inch cock and stroked it in rhythm. She dropped to her knees and slurped his prick for a while, a sight I admired. She had worn a long pencil skirt and tight white blouse. Rod lifted her skirt up to reveal her multi-colored string bikini panties.

Soon Rod stripped her down and placed her on the bed, positioning himself behind her ass. He wanted to admire her famous booty and licked his lips in anticipation. To my and her surprise he darted his tongue and licked her ass; she giggled and squirmed in delight as a fire began in her loins. She mounted him thereafter and slid down his long ten inches with no hesitation. It was the first time and I think the longest and hardest she had ever ridden anyone so big. They fucked hard and he had her turn around and screw him—still on top but facing away. Her tits bounced and her huge nipples were erect. "This is my praying mantis posture," he blurted out. He had her place her arms back and to the sides of the bed. They banged even more with her facing this way. I watched my wanton young wife riding his long black pole and loving every minute of it

They were passionate and she was attracted to him. He turned her missionary, and they long-dicked for an hour. She came heavily. His dreads bounced on her face, and she squealed in utter delight. He turned her around, slapped her bubble butt, and fucked her doggie style. I think she came again. They eventually switched back to face-to-face fucking, and he came on her stomach. Later she appeared to be satisfied and done, but he came out of the bathroom ready for more. Rod had a joint, and it had been years since Sara had touched the stuff. He got her high and horny again and soon enough she slipped out of her lounge pants and let him move her into a wild sixty-nine posture. He was hard again in no time and wanting more action.

Sliding a new condom on Rod had her passionate again. He was only able to get the condom halfway down before she got on him and slid onto his prick. This time her riding session topped the first. Newly inspired passion made the action wildly rough. I watched as she bounced heavily up and down, moaning loudly and coming hard. "Ohhhhh, hooooly shit, ummmm," she screamed out, as they kept pounding away.

I recall thinking that this is the hardest I had ever seen my beloved wife screw. He would last all night, and she would bounce all night. She came again. While watching this cowgirl action, I recalled an article I had read. It said that deep penetration could actually tap the cervix of a woman, and the cervix is known to have the most sensitive nerve endings in a woman's vagina. This rang true in Sara's case; she was out of her mind.

We had accidently left the sunroof open, and a rainstorm had soaked the interior of our car. We laughed as we sat in our wet car before pulling out of the hotel parking lot.

We drove home happy and chatted along the drive. "He was good," she said, yet I sensed desire to see Tyron still in her voice. After we got home she insisted on writing a review on Rod's online profile page. The comment was something like this: "He was hot from the start, sexy and hard. He bounced me off the walls with orgasm after orgasm. I look forward to our next encounter." Despite this great five-star review, I knew Tyron was still on her mind. My wife was truly a hotwife now. She had experienced sublimely good sex and deep intimate moments of passion. My work would be cut out for me now. I had to keep up the pace and keep her happy and enjoying her newfound hotness.

The next day I placed a new personal ad. The header of the profile read as follows: "Happily married blond baby-doll seeking her stud. Wife has model looks and can never get enough hardcore sex. Men reading this please be fairly tall, good-looking and very well hung. She prefers black men who know how to satisfy a young passionate woman. Husband watches only."

I had to make sure the next guy was a winner and good for her, if not, there would be no avoiding another meet with her preferred lover.

I contacted Lando, a tall black guy a few states away, and we began making plans to meet. He seemed fit for the job; another couple had highly recommended him. In the meantime life went on and went through some changes. At sporting events and the health club, I found myself stealing looks at other men's cocks. By no mean am I bi-sexual; I just wanted to see if there were any that would be right for lovely Sara. At the health club the cocks in the showers were mostly smaller and attached to older men. I saw nothing great. In our mainly white-skinned state, the Caucasians were small to average size in the dong department. Every so often a large penis would turn up and my groin would stir as I thought about this chap with my wife—how he would be large enough to fill her and make her moan. Once I met a lawyer with a thick mushroom-headed specimen. He pranced in the shower, heads above the other small men, a suit-and-tie fellow. I wanted to find a way to match them up, to offer my little blond to him. Perhaps we needed some business-related attorney help. I ran it through my fantastical mind for days. Nothing came of it. Our positions in the community were too high, and there was no way I could let it leak out what we did on the side. Our families and co-workers would be traumatized.

    In the coming weeks, I dealt with some missed chances. We tried out a few more local white guys. These were not good encounters. I should never have initiated them. Sara did not like these men. We had no sexual chemistry and, later in the evening, no sexual play. I was to be her man those nights, and I had pretty big shoes to fill. I decided it was time to buy Viagra from Canada. I also invested in new sex toys like rubber cock rings and girth enhancers for myself. It would have to do, but I was no substitute for a good encounter with a sexy hung black man. As Sara said more than once, "I like the three-hour sessions. I like it hard and deep, too." Those words lingered in my mind as I searched nightly online for better men to meet.

    One night I tried out the girth enhancers. I slipped the thick cock ring over my thin member, covering it from the bottom way up its tallest peak. My cock got squeezed tight and blood pumped to make it hard. I downed the Viagra and felt like maybe I would be able to perform. As I entered her—hard and thicker for once—she was on fire. My wife said, "Oh baby, you feel so good tonight honey. Give it to me hard, deep, make me feel like a woman." I did my best but I lasted only ten minutes and she was still horny. She sprawled on the bed, masturbating, asking me to lick her pussy, to fondle her thick nipples, and to finger her clit. She wanted more, and called out to anyone listening, "I'm so horny! I need more."

Next we met a couple. It so happened that they were in the area and wanted to hit a strip club we had also heard was nice. Perhaps we all could hook up with studs for the ladies. With that in mind, we decided to try meeting up with them and hitting the club. The couple was attractive, and we hit it off enough to join them at the exotic dancer club. There we watched sexy ladies dance and listened to wild rock music. The female half of the couple was really into the ladies. I was hoping she'd be into looking for men at the club, but we ended up with several couples' lap dances and just women around us most of the night.

It was amazing having all the best-looking dancers do private dances for the four of us. I really admire these attractive ladies. They know how to make a man melt, so confident are they in their dancing and gorgeous nude bodies. In this case they had our wives melting too.

We managed to leave early enough to go to a local club where I heard many black men visited, but the club was sparsely attended and no one excited the ladies. We all ended up back at our hotel. The ladies were horny so they made out and played some. The guy was watching Sara as the ladies played and I suggested he join them. As his wife Sasha was eating Sara out and had her on her knees, I recall him saying, "Oh man, look at those puffy wide-open lips. She is incredible." Sasha had Sara all worked up. She wanted a cock—*that* I knew. When Tim came around and fondled her breasts, he roused her even more. She was unbuckling his pants in what was supposed to be all girl-on-girl action. He pulled out a magnum condom and undressed. He was nowhere near the size of some of the black guys we had met. He entered my wife with one push. Sasha sat back on a chair and masturbated. Then she, too, was hot for more action and joined back in.

This couple enjoyed Sara's hot body. The man did get Sara yelping in pleasure, yet the sex was nothing special. He was not that big and she took him easily and without much effort. Later that night we talked about the fun we'd had but again, she was disappointed no studs had been around.

The guy from the couple reminded me of the one we had used as a last-minute replacement the night we were supposed to meet the exceptional black trucker at a bar. Sara had said a few things that night as they had fucked, words that still rang in my mind: "Oh, am I horny!" He had asked her how she wanted it and as she got on his cock she had said," I want it hard, real hard and deep." After trying to fuck her as hard as he could with his rather small penis he turned her over and asked if she would prefer it with him on top. She stroked her clit and said," I want it hard, much harder and I'm so wet." It was so obvious she needed bigger.

The several times we had not found what we wanted took a toll on us. We were spending too much money on babysitters, and lots of money and time were being diverted from other important activities. We got frustrated with each other when party nights were foiled or the action was only so-so. Our marriage did not need the stress.

Chapter Seven

At least Lando had made plans to come up. We heard good things about him being a tall, well-endowed stud. In the meantime I wondered how men with huge cocks lived a normal life. Having a small dick was easy; you never thought about sharing it with sexy beautiful girls you saw at work or play. A tiny wang was nothing to be proud of, and a soft one even worse. No high-quality woman wanted a teeny one. How could a guy like the monster-cocked older guy Ken we had met a while back live normally? His tool was so big that the sensations he experienced whenever he saw a sexy lady any day of the week must have made it overwhelmingly difficult to focus on day-to-day living.

He could impress anyone he got naked with and was constantly hard as a rock. We all know woman turn men on every second of the day. We want to fuck all the women who look good; it's natural. I thought of how a guy like that lived and sometimes thought it wasn't so bad being small—might save a lot of aggravation in life. I chuckle whenever thoughts like these come to mind.

We picked the coldest night of winter to meet Lando. We had a quick dinner and ran to our hotel room to escape the wind chill. He was decent-enough looking, but not overly special. I think Sara was semi-attracted to Lando; she was so picky and knew so quickly whether it was a go or not that I worried. We were both so highly stressed when seeing and meeting a new guy that it was almost too much to handle. She was a *yes* or *no* and that was it—five hundred miles of travel or not, it didn't matter. *I think we need a new plan*, I would often say to myself when we were about to meet a new guy after a long road trip.

Luckily they talked and laughed. She sipped some wine and slipped out of her skirt and danced about on the hotel bed in black thigh-high stockings and sexy black-thong panties. Soon she was embracing him as he stood above her, tall and excited. She undid his pants and gave him a smooth blowjob. I was jealous that I never got head. She slurped him good and he got hard. Lando was not as big as I had hoped, but he was at least medium. There appeared to be no one who could compare to Tryon these days in getting the wife hot, but she was ready for good sex. We had had very little in past months.

He ate her half-shaven silky-soft pussy, and she was wet and juicy for a real dicking. It was cold outside but heating up within. He got on top of her and pushed in. She squealed with delight, taking all of him right off. They fucked hard and in unison. She began touching her clit, reaching down for more satisfaction and soon achieving an explosive orgasm. She liked the screwing. He took her from behind then got on top and took her again. She came and moaned in delight. They both fell to the bed, tired and sweating from each other's body heat.

He wanted more, but Sara was happy to call it a night. This was a prime example of her liking the sex but not being overly interested in the guy; he was not setting her on fire with lust and attraction. If that had been the case, she would have kept going. Lando, however, made another move. He slipped down the thin blanket that covered Sara on the hotel bed and ate her pussy again. He then licked at her swollen cunt lips and tickled her clit. Suddenly she came to life. I watched as she checked his cock for hardness. Like most studs we have met he was rock hard and ready.

He suddenly stood up, pulled her up in the air and swung her upside down. It was a standing sixty-nine, the first I had ever seen live, and the first Sara had ever experienced. She said, "What are you doing, oh Lord." He held her firm like a real stud and licked her swollen, now burning cunt. It wasn't long before he laid her back down on the bed. He rolled her onto him, and she was more than happy to play.

She climbed on and rode his prick. She bounced about and soon he rolled her over for another missionary, pushing into her steady and fast. Sara groaned loudly and again played with her clit until she reached orgasm. He pulled out and came and the night came to an end.

"He was fun," she said on the long ride home. "Maybe we could meet him again someday." Then, about one minute later, she added that he was above average, and maybe another meet could happen as long as it took place after a second Tyron meet.

We had never met anyone more than once, so this talk of a second meet with any guy was huge in the conversation department. Our swinging lifestyle had never reached this point, and I really did not want it to. The last thing I wanted was for her to be overly attracted to one guy. I preferred new large dick for her; the newness of an encounter was part of the thrill for me. Plus, she was not as likely to fall for one guy and always compare him to whoever we'd meet in the future. Sara claimed that the more sex she had, the more she wanted sex; it was making her ultra horny fucking so much.

There was no one new to meet at the moment. So we had to deal with home play. I got her a new glass dildo and decided that Viagra was the drug for me. I'd at least be able to give her some sex in between meets. I made it a point to purchase a forty-eight pack of magnum extra-large condoms so we'd have enough in stock for the times to come. I also got Sara a new book on CD called *How to Make Love to a Man*. She really took to it, studying ways to give head and even how to put a condom on a guy. These were all new events for us, and things were still looking up as for our open lifestyle. I desired no other women, only wanting my wife to have as much sex as a younger woman with such a capacity could desire. You may think Sara was easy, or better yet, a whore. This was not the case. She was actually quite innocent. Perhaps one would think her a poor obedient woman? Not at all. She is a very successful lady—highly educated and well off. She has never cheated on me or given me any reason to suspect her of cheating. And yet, if any of her family or co-workers had known what we were up to, they would have been shocked.

During the months that followed, I could not locate any tall slim well-hung black studs who were Sara's type. We had met one hot black stud online, and Sara and he had chatted on the phone, building up a great degree of lust prior to our planned meeting. But he canceled his flight to come to our city at the last minute. Sara was not happy and began asking to meet Tyron again.

I rushed us into another couples' meet-up. A mixed couple was in the area for a wine festival, and we ended up joining them at the event. We went out dancing after and found ourselves back at the hotel room. The guy was black and good-looking enough to interest Sara. His wife was a little snooty and not all that great. She was into Sara, and the two got along well enough to join us. They both wanted to sample Sara together, so we invited them to our room. The woman undressed Sara and licked her shaven pussy while her husband watched. He soon joined in, and together they both got between Sara's silky thighs. The couple licked away at my wife's hot cunt, smiles on both their faces. The wife would not let her husband fuck Sara; they only played and licked her entire body. Sara was craving a fucking—that I could tell—but the fun ended there.

It had been another enjoyable yet unsatisfying night overall. My wife needed a huge stud to pound her big pussy and we had not had that. Sara told me she would have fucked the guy if his wife had been up for it.

Our lives flew by and we met no one for some time. Over the next few months, I turned to white guys for possibles. We had exhausted our supply of black studs anywhere nearby and at the time we did not travel enough to consider other choices. Hundreds of white men answered our newest ad. We turned down almost all of them.

So many men were nuts over my wife's pics. They wanted her and offered us everything from trips to sports games to concerts to exotic vacations for a chance to "party" with sexy Sara. I was not jealous; having a wife who is seen by other men as sexually "hot" was a great ego booster.

We met one such guy named Alex at a restaurant on a Saturday night. From corresponding online earlier in the week via a personals ad, I knew he was young, in shape and well hung. He was craving to be with an older woman and Sara fit that bill, even though she was only in her early thirties. As soon as we walked into the place, I knew Sara was not happy. He was too thin, too clean and too preppy for her. She was not attracted. Here we were several cities away from home, with a hotel room and a guy who could fuck her silly, and yet she was not interested.

After dinner I gave them time alone to dance at a nearby club, but nothing would change her mind. He was upset and asked why no fun. We explained that it took an attraction for her to want to play and that she was not easy to please.

That night was the beginning of what would be a constant fight over the next three years whenever we considered meeting a new man. It seemed like we would not find anyone else that great; it was starting to affect our swinging nights out. We needed a new plan. White guys simply did not turn her on.

I decided that meeting another white guy would probably not work out. It was always a crapshoot with my wife. There was only one thing left to try. I decided we'd host a black and white interracial party for several black studs and several white couples at a hotel. We'd do it in a state in between places where there were lots of good candidates. This way Sara could look over all the guys in advance, and then we could hook up with one that night or make plans for an encounter on another weekend. The party was scheduled, and we found nine studs and five couples to attend. We booked a large multi-suite room at a hotel in a central location for all the people involved and set a date. I thought, *Why didn't I think of this before?*

In the meantime, I was corresponding with Tyron online a lot. He was ready to meet again and anxious to have my wife once more. He described the things about her he liked and compared her favorably to the hundreds of other wives and girlfriends he had enjoyed over the years. He of course mentioned her long curly blond locks again. He liked the way they flowed freely about her pretty face and draped over her eyes during times of great passion. He had met few ladies with such wonderful hair. She was also younger than most wives so she had a mindsct similar to his own. He also mentioned that her ass was the kind he truly liked. He loved a round bubbly butt, could not deal with a flat ass. He wanted some meat, an ass that was firm but well rounded. We both knew Sara had that. He liked her body, her large nipples and her passion for long hours of sexual play. He told me again that he rated her in his top ten, in fact top five. I was thinking wow, *my little Sara is a winner—a top-five hotwife*. I also was thinking, *Damn, this guy has bedded way too many chicks.*

With all the stress of meeting poor choices and not finding good studs, both Sara and I had long conversations about our lifestyle. Because she was really into Tyron and hoping to meet him again, she was willing to consider other meets. But in truth, I developed a sense that if not for him she would have been too frustrated to continue swinging. It was all about the guy being major hot; otherwise she had a hard time dealing with it all. We talked again about finding a full time lover for her—a special once-a-month fuck buddy we could welcome into our intimate mix. He would enjoy her a lot and they would become real lovers. I had a hard time with that idea, so it never flew.

She needed more sex, deeper penetration, more hardcore banging, and we were having a hard time making that happen. I worked on finding great black guys for the upcoming interracial party, which was coming together just fine. If we could just meet some great guys, everything would be perfect. She felt no guilt if the guys were winners. A winner to her was simply a hot looking tall lean well-hung black guy. There were none left anywhere near our rural location.

We continued to talk about whether to keep swinging. Sara's Catholic upbringing was making her feel like perhaps the whole scene was too overwhelming for her spirit. Then came days when we'd watch basketball and a sexy black ball player would enter the court and she'd say, "Wow, he's so hot. I wish we could party with him." So there was never a dull moment for us. Her body was saying *yes*, but her mind was saying *no more*.

The big party was coming up and I did all I could to arrange for good people to attend. A tall sexy basketball player was coming who I felt would be a good choice. I also had a sort of naughty boy coming whose good looks I imagined Sara would find hot. Both these guys were built and black. One of the guys was bringing a so-called cool cousin I knew little about. There were others attending as well, a guy who—according to his online pics—looked well built and solid, plus another I had high hopes for—a dark-skinned, bald, tattooed fellow. All of them were black. As for couples, we found four others, all with sexy slim wives that adored black cock. It looked like it would be one heck of a party.

The idea of couples like us with attractive wives who loved swinging and enjoyed black men was very appealing after everything we had been doing on our own over the years.

The problems began when a big winter storm came in the day before Saturday's bash. We had picked a central location for all the gang, but that still meant a two-hour drive for most. Two of the couples were snowed in and had to cancel their trip. It was the day of party, and this was not good news. Nine black studs were still attending, and we were down to three couples. I scrambled to get at least one other couple, and it seemed as if I had. I had very little prior knowledge of them and hated to take this route, but I had no choice.

We had one older couple who claimed the wife could take on the whole crew of men if need be. The remaining couples had far less adventurous wives. Sara had never been with more than one guy at a time so she, too, would not be the crowd entertainer for the party.

It was the night of the party, and we were on our way. On the drive another couple called and cancelcd. We were now down to just three or four couples. One was the new couple we knew little about. We arrived safely and met the older couple first. They seemed nice enough. She was a horny one for sure, but did not look like her younger pictures. I knew the guys would bang her but not be overly crazy about it. I debated calling to cancel some of the men, but clung to the hope that all the couples would arrive.

But no others did. The men arrived on time, all of them. My plan to arrange for Sara to meet a roomful of black dongs was happening—but not the way I expected. We played some party music on our iPods and offered a few basic snacks. All the guys were friendly enough and Sara found one named Dante to her liking. I met a taller basketball player named Hank who was pretty cool, too, and we talked sports. It was nice to meet him. Luckily for us the other older wife entertained a few of the guys in one of the two big bedrooms early on. An hour in another couple arrived—the new one we knew little about. She was a sexy, slim older blond with short hair but a real nice body—classy looking and ready for fun. Her husband, however, seemed stuffy; it turned out they only wanted one black guy. Her husband had to join in, and they wanted the door closed in the other bedroom for privacy.

This was not so good. Having three men to join in the play was a start, but then no couples came. There were nine men in all. The rest of the crew played cards with Sara. She did like Dante; he was personable, sexy and thankfully her type.

Dante's cousin seemed fairly cool, too. He was short, yet attractive and solid. The other guys were all okay, nothing special, though one was built well; his face, however, did not get Sara going. The tall basketball player and I chatted away.

I wanted to lose some of the guys because we had no lady for them but did not know how to do so just yet. Luckily the older woman invited a few into the other bedroom. At least they had some fun. I pulled Sara aside and we discussed what we should do and how she felt about it all.

She liked Dante and said she would like to have him before the night was over. He wanted his cousin, too. She thought the tall basketball guy was cute, too—maybe another time. As for the rest, she wanted to get rid of them. We felt bad that there were not enough couples. So we let it ride some, played cards, listened to music, and let the guys play with the older wife in one of the suite rooms with an open door policy. Hank, the tall basketball player, mostly talked to me but had his eye on Sara the whole night. We did our best to push things along and eventually most of the guys left. I told Hank that she was interested—just not tonight. That way we had some good options for another time. The party idea actually was working out okay. No one caught Sara's eye other than Dante and his cousin so we had them stay over.

Once everyone was gone, the party began in earnest. Sara was excited, but she had never been with two guys before so I had no idea how things would unfold. She wanted to dance, so I got some music ready. She changed into a revealing semi-see-through sexy lingerie fishnet outfit. The guys were like, *wow!* She paraded about in this transparent red camisole. She was on fire. It did not take long before she was in full tease mode, dancing and fondling the guys. Both black guys loved the entertainment. She played with their cocks and dazzled them with her moves. Her plump round butt was grooving and her lush long thick curly blond hair was flowing to the sound of the tunes.

She could wait no longer and pulled Dante into a bedroom. His cousin would have to wait. *Be patient*, I told him. After they entered the room, I slipped in to see them pushed up against the wall, making out. They passionately kissed and she was already aflame with desire. She unzipped his pants to reveal a very long, thick cock. Seconds after my wife began to stroke him, he was erect.

They moved to the bed and got naked rather quickly. She slurped his cock like she never did for me and was soon urging him to *fuck her good*. But his cousin could wait no longer; he came in the room. I was like, *oh no, he should have waited his turn*. When he took his clothes off, I saw that he had a small penis. He wanted attention and urged Sara to give him head. She blew him some but was more into Dante for sure. The cousin, who was not even hard, had to stand back.

Dante took over. He pushed Sara onto her back and entered her. She moaned loudly and said, "Oh baby, this is what I need. Give it to me, make me cum." He fucked her passionately and they moved together—a great fit. The cousin wanted in and kept trying to get involved. He was soft and small, and she barely noticed him.

Dante fucked her doggy style. Again the cousin placed his small cock in her mouth, but she was not into it. He got frustrated and left the room. I was happy when Dante seized the opportunity to pound Sara onto her back again. She loved it! I overheard her say, "This feels so good; I can't get enough of you."

But the cousin came back and wanted his turn. Dante pulled away and let him in but he was still soft and Sara seemed frustrated. I had to step in and say we should call it a night. The cousin got angry. There was almost a fight, but things cooled down. Do you think a cuckold husband can fight? I might have found out.

After this encounter, my big fantasy of Sara in a gangbang situation seemed far off. My loving wife was not a slut. She liked one guy at a time. I had imagined her a little more wild—maybe with a few tattoos, a more sluttish style. That would not be the case. I had at least hoped she'd do a double penetration. Anyway, we cleaned up the hotel suite and prepared to head out.

Dante was in the hallway, and I saw Sara run out to give him a huge hug. We packed up and decided to drive home that very night. It was, overall, an interesting party. We met a few cool people, but mostly no one promising for the future. We planned a future meet with Hank that we both knew would be a worthwhile encounter, so the drive home was a decent one. Sara sang along with the radio, and when the announcer paused, she said, "That tall guy you kept talking with I kind of liked. I'd meet him some night."

The storm and somewhat disappointing party saddened my Florida friend Jose as well. A cuckold wannabe, he offered to fly us as a couple to Miami, Florida. The city is considered the essence of hotness. The plan was as follows: we fly first class to Miami—all on him. We would meet up, and he would take Sara on a shopping spree to the sexiest and most upscale clothing stores on Ocean Drive. Our hotel would be the finest in South Beach. Sara would be pampered with manicures and pedicures and all that jazz later in the afternoon. In the evening he would take us to the hottest clubs in the city.

The catch was this: prior to our arrival, he would line up black studs for us to meet. Pre-approved men who fit Sara's desires. Her requirements were simple: tall, well-endowed, great-looking, fit black men with class. The trip was in the works. Sara loved the idea; she had never had a chance to travel, and this was one heck of an opportunity. Hopefully it would come to fruition sometime in the near future. My online friend had a hot Latino wife and was dying to open up their marriage. He was poorly endowed and ready to become a full-fledged cuckold. He told me he would love the humiliation. I did not really like to be made into a submissive, but Sara probably could have gotten anything she wanted out of me at this time.

As the weeks went by, we knew Hank would be our next meet. In truth we did not consider the typical *who do we meet now?* question. Instead our main thought was, *how do we avoid a terrible encounter with a guy?* We made plans to meet Hank in a few months. Our sex life continued to be okay at best. She had experienced a large cock and craved it. I could not stay hard for long, and with my small size, the lovemaking was fair at best. We loved each other and at least that carried us onward. This was emotionally wrenching for me, too. There were many times after meeting a guy that I felt we should take a break from all of this stuff. The entire process was draining.

I kept talking with my fellow cuckold friend online. A well-to-do married chap from Miami, he took great interest in my wife and our exploits and we became good friends. Eventually I even let him talk to Sara on the phone. Jose was really into the black guy/white wife thing. He had a sexy wife himself but had yet to get her into the lifestyle. He was so ready for it that it drove him nuts. He sort of adopted my wife as his fantasy hotwife.

He begged to see pics of my baby doll, so I would show him a few shots here and there and he would masturbate to them. Jose would even go so far as to buy sexy lingerie for Sara, as well as bikini panties and high heel shoes. We would shop together online at Victoria's Secret. He truly loved his new online friend and my beautiful wife. He wanted her to have the best. Whenever he could, he would send her lovely, expensive items. I would secretly show him shots of my wife in the arms of these men. At the sight of the contrasting skin of the guys' large cocks pressed up against her, he would go absolutely nuts and jerk off on the spot. I recall him going off one night while I shared a picture of Sara with a stud. "Oh wow, she's wearing the beige bra and panty set I sent her. How awesome!" I loved his reactions. He would often say stuff like, "It is so amazing seeing these muscular, well-hung, giant-dick-wielding men with your little wife. She is the best, and you have given her the finest."

Sara kept asking to meet Tyron. I was beginning to get the feeling we'd have to do it or our swinging days would be limited. I suggested we take some new pictures to show him. She liked the idea of giving him something to lead up to the meeting. We planned a shoot that weekend.

That week I made it a point to watch my favorite films. I always enjoyed *Unfaithful* with Richard Gere and *Eyes Wide Shut* with Ted Cruise. There was one other movie called the *Voyeur* that I also liked. All three movies depicted sexy open-marriage type pleasures.

A fantasy had lingered in my mind all week. I thought about hiding in the closet during our next encounter. Sara would meet the stud at the bar below in the lobby of our hotel. She would tell the guy her husband had decided to go see a movie instead of joining in. Then, upstairs in our room, they would arrive as a couple—no hubby in sight. In my mind this would free the guy to act as he liked. He would not hold back out of worry that a husband's eye was on him. I envisioned him taking my petite wife and doing as he pleased. He would be rough and make her beg harder for more vivid sexual play. I could only hope that one day this would become a reality. I knew these men had to be holding back. I mean, a husband was there watching intently over his prized wife!

The weekend came and we arranged to take the photos in private. Now, seeing that these photos were supposed to entice Tyron to meet us as soon as possible, Sara became a different model, one whose animal instincts were on full display. She posed with an enthusiasm I had never before witnessed. Her smile expressed wanton lust. In the poses, she rolled a finger, beckoning the viewer to come forward. She arched her back more than ever and stuck her ass out to make it seem more defined. She teased the camera, wanting the results to be excellent.

She did one thing that was a first; she opened her legs during some of the pics. I was simply amazed. This girl was on fire. Her puffy pussy lips were in pictures for the first time. This woman has big lips and when aroused, they grew larger and more open, fully exposing her wide cunt-opening to the camera. We took shots of her in sexy lingerie, exposing her breasts in several shots—her pierced belly button, her plump ass, and of course her amazingly pretty face. She danced and posed with vigor. She put on high-heeled boots, garter belts and more. Her smile was infectious. We ended up with some of the best pictures I had ever taken. She even grabbed her coveted black dildo and posed with that too. I took that out when she posed for the last set of pics. I knew she was aroused by the others and the thought of who would be seeing them. She grabbed her toy and masturbated with a zest.

Jose my online buddy was also shocked. He was like, *what has gotten into her?* I mean, all the past pics we had taken to seduce and lure men into meeting had all been great. We had taken classy, well-done pics; yet these new shots had a whole new look to them: her face was lit up. I was like, *yes indeed. I need to up my Viagra intake.* If you have never taken the drug, let me say it works. As the days had gone by, then the years, I had become in my forties much less potent. My cock felt different—softer, smaller and less excited. I wished it had been different but it's wasn't.

The drug Viagra, which Hugh Hefner calls the greatest achievement of mankind, works. I would get hard from it and last longer.

As summer approached we ended up meeting a really cool couple who hosted parties nearby. This was great, because we didn't have to travel so far. The guy's wife liked men, too, so we could invite everyone we knew to the parties. Hank was our first invite along with two other black men we had been corresponding with during the months that followed our newest photo shoot.

The couple had a gorgeous, huge home. Several couples and the black guys were invited for a steamy bash one future weekend. We knew Sara liked Hank's look. Other men had also been invited, so everything was looking good. I did not care for tons of couples, but they, too, had been invited. The party was planned and we had something to look forward to. Back at home I decided to give a few new things a try. I bought a strap-on hollow dildo of good size and thought that it just might be the marital tool that could jump-start our sex life. I also picked up some adult DVDs that Sara actually liked to watch.

Sara also dug out the audio book I had gotten not too much earlier: *How to make Love to a Man*. It worked best in her car when driving back and forth to work. She would tell me about what it had taught her. The first thing was how to stroke a cock. She spoke about the wrist motion and how to rotate one's hand to continue stroking without letting go. She wanted to practice on me and I was like, *All right I guess*. The biggest find on her end was the condom putting-on section. She had found a way to put a condom on with her mouth— a trick neither of us had mastered. One evening she tried her skills on me. The stroke was cool and she was finally able to get me hard. She placed the condom—a normal sized Trojan—in her mouth and slid it over my cock rather smoothly. I was impressed. She, too, was giddy over her newfound talent. She said with great enthusiasm, "I can't wait to show Tyron this." I was not surprised, and made it a point to peek upstairs at the black dildo and pics of them together that I had strategically placed in order on the closet shelf. I'd have bet my life that the dong and pics had been moved as usual and used vigorously by my horny wife for playtime and masturbation. I checked and—low and behold—all had been disturbed. Almost every time I checked, they had been moved.

The strap-on big hollow rubber dildo was next on the agenda. It was skin-like and huge. I was able to place it over my small prick easily; the straps encased my pubic region and butt. If I was hard or not, it would not matter. I could give Sara all she wanted and fuck her for hours. One evening I slipped it on during a moment when she was soaking wet and craving great sex. I was very excited to be able to have long deep sex with her, yet she seemed tense as I mounted her. I pushed into her and she gulped—a first for me. I was throbbing inside the thick nine-inch hollow sleeve. She tried to roll with it but asked me to stop. I pulled away and she was like, "I don't want that thing. I like the feel of a real, warm cock." I was utterly disappointed. I went soft the rest of the night. She tried a blowjob on me for the first time in years. That, too, failed.

The party that our newfound friends Ted and Taja were co-hosting could not come soon enough. Sara was a knockout as usual. She wore a jean miniskirt, a tight white blouse and a cowboy hat. Her finger and toenails were pretty pink. Hank was supposed to be there, so we both knew a tall, fit, handsome black male would grace the grounds. All was good.

Ted and Taja's house was stunning—ritzy and spacious to the core. The floors were all hardwood, and the place had three levels to play in. The main room was furnished with a sleek bar and a big dining room, open at the other end. A floor made for dancing dominated the center of the main room with a balcony above. We took a look downstairs. It, too, was graced with beauty—leather couches, chairs and a big pool table, not to mention a giant flat-screen TV. All areas had private playrooms, too. The main floor had a big master bedroom, the loft a futon and chairs, and downstairs there were two more separate private bedrooms. This place was a swinger's paradise.

The guests began arriving promptly, and we were all excited. The couples were first to arrive. Most were attractive, yet the men were not Sara's type. She liked studs, young studs. These guys were around my age—40s and decent enough, yet not what she desired for sexual play. I found many of the ladies quite lovely. Some were fit and sexy. The couples, however, were looking to meet other couples, and this was not our thing. We felt sort of like outcasts. However, we did talk, laugh and have fun. Taja, at least, liked single men, so things were fine.

The problem was that no single guys had shown up. We had invited four—one being Hank from the interracial party we had hosted. The others were new men we had met online. Another Ted knew from a meet he and his wife had enjoyed. The couples danced and frolicked about. We, too, made the best of it, wondering where the hell the men were. This one thing—no hot single men—would work against us for many parties to come. The location was too rural, too far away from the big city, and after this initial party things would not get that much better.

Couples make it a point to find good quality upscale friends to party with; they entertain themselves on long road trips. Single men, we soon learned, were a different breed. They liked short drives, easy trips and quick hits. By ten no guys had shown up, and the couples all began getting wild in rooms throughout the house.

Sara was not happy. We watched as four naked bodies entered the master bedroom and rolled about, enjoying a foursome. I tried to cheer her up, playing with her body and looking for arousal, but there was none. My cellphone rang and, low and behold, Hank was on the other end. "I'm on my way. I had a flat tire but am coming soon." This was good news. When I relayed it to the wife she was like, *thank God*. A small smile came up on her pouty, pink-glossed lips.

Hank finally arrived and it took very little time for Sara to drag him up to the loft area. He looked good—very tall, perhaps 6'6", I would guess. He was lean and wearing sporty clothes, designer sweatpants and a pullover shirt. I grabbed my camera bag and followed the new couple up the stairway. She kneeled there, already pulling his sweats down, exposing his cock and sucking him furiously. She was ready to party.

Hank was a big guy in height and stature, but his penis was average. He was big enough to be there and she was as horny as hell, yet I knew it would be only a decent encounter as soon as I saw what he was packing. They moved to the futon. Sara slipped out of her little cowgirl outfit, and he went directly for her pussy and began an eating-out session. It took a few minutes, but he got between her legs quite soon and pushed in with one thrust. They banged in the loft, on the futon, seriously squeezing each other tight.

A few people wandered in to take a peek. The tall black guy and the small, pale, tiny white wife was the main attraction. Sara's big protruding nipples were sprung out and she took all Hank could give, pulling his ass into her. Ted and Taja came up to look, too. Sara held back her cries of lust, yet could not contain herself at one point, moaning, "Give me all you got. Yes, oh yes, do me." Later Ted would say, "Mitch, you know that guy was not all that big. I thought you said she liked her men real large. One of the guys who was a no-show is much bigger. We'll have to make sure he comes to the next party."

I was like, *absolutely*.

There was no real major attraction with Hank as it turned out. Their sexual fling ended quickly. Sara did not want anymore. We all chatted downstairs and eventually picked up the mess and bid farewell.

    We both talked about how there needed to be more hot men at the next party. I gulped down Viagra on the drive back home and was able to get hard for her before we went to sleep. She was horny and wanted much more.

Chapter Eight

As the weeks passed, we met no one. Winter settled in, and Sara insisted that we should meet Tyron again. I told her we'd choose a date soon. In the meantime I met a fellow online who was back from military duty and somewhat local. He was a light-skinned black whose picture Sara had seen once and found attractive. He offered to meet us nearby at a bar. I asked the wife if she was up for it. A guy who lived nearby and was a good prospect was a gift, and I did not want to pass up this great opportunity.

She was pretty well fixated on the upcoming Tyron meet but was willing to talk to Don on the phone. I arranged for a phone conversation. They chatted one Friday evening, and I was surprised at how well the talk went. I overheard Sara saying, "Well you have me all excited now." In the end she was up for a meeting. In fact, a Saturday-night encounter was planned for that weekend. We rushed to get a sitter and made reservations at a hotel nearby. Sizzling things were set in motion. Saturday could not come soon enough.

The short drive to the restaurant, which had a bar area for eating and drinking, was easy enough. Sara wore a brown and white lace miniskirt that was really hot. A thin white tight-fitting sweater was her top of choice. She slipped on some white thigh-highs and added long white fur points to the ensemble. She was a playboy bunny, and Don was sure to be pleased.

I knew that under it all she was wearing a bra and panty set I had picked up for her earlier in the week. It made sense; it was a camo and pink combo thong and bra set. The guy was in the service, so how cool was that? We found Don in the lounge right away and introductions were made. He wasn't very tall, yet he was decent-looking, military proud with a close-shaved haircut, nice dress pants and shirt. He was a mix of white and black, and Sara liked what she saw. We moved to a table and ordered drinks. Don seemed nice enough. The question was, would Sara find him truly sexy? She was not one to fake it, either an attraction was there or the night was going to end badly. We talked and he flirted with her at the table. I noticed he placed his hand under the table and fondled her inner thigh. The touching was a good thing and always got Sara in the mood. She seemed to like this guy and they touched and flirted while we sipped our drinks.

    I felt they had chemistry and suggested outright that we head to our hotel room next door and keep the party going. They both agreed and out we went. When we arrived in the suite Don wasted no time engaging my hot wife in petting. He kissed her and grabbed her ass. I frantically tried to get my video recorder up and running, as the man pulled up her skirt, exposing her thong. He unclipped her bra, too, and there she stood, braless, her long blond hair running down her back, thong and white fishnet thigh-highs in full view. He pushed her to the bed and they embraced. He slipped his shirt off and pants too. They kissed and hugged, rolling about the bed. I had my camera running, finally.

    She made her way into his shorts, revealing his penis. I was like *wow, we are in for one hot night*. This guy was hung big and thick. Close to the largest guy we'd ever met. Fondling my hotwife got him stiff in seconds. He loved her wild, curly blond hair all over his body. Her bubble butt was pushing and pumping into his loins. His giant prick was curved heavily in one direction and stood hard, proud, and ready for duty.

    They kissed and melted into each other. She climbed on him and I wondered what she was doing. She was very aggressive, and I thought *holy shit* she might take him into her condom-less. But she was only teasing and eventually got off him and prepared for her new condom placement trick. Sara had worked quite a while on this place-a–condom-on-with-your-mouth trick at home, but this was the first time she'd actually tried it in this type of situation. She grabbed an extra large Trojan magnum from the bedside, unwrapped it, and put it in her mouth; then came the true test of her skills. She tried to lower the condom on to his big thick dong, but unlike at home, she could not slide it down his huge shaft. He was too big, too wide. She had practiced on her thin vibrator and my small dick; these were easy targets. His dick was almost as wide as a Pepsi can and the condom only went on at its tip. She was disappointed.

In the end Don showed her how to get the condom on. He pulled the material wide open—like opening a Ziploc baggie—then placed it over his cock. There was no way a condom—even an extra large one—would just slide down his member. Sara had picked the wrong guy for her first demonstration of "mouth-putting-on" technique. She was, however, happy and ready for action. I put on some better music and went to get them water. I was playing the dutiful cuckold, serving the wife and her hung lover. When I glanced over, he was hard-as-a-rock ready.

Sara swayed to the new song, "Fuck you like an Animal," and the real party was about to begin. Now that he was outfitted, she wasted no time jumping back on him. Her cheeky ass bounced about and they kissed some more, pressing together. Her nipples protruded fiercely; she was searing hot. She positioned herself over his dong and slid the head into her now moist pussy lips. She was throbbing open now and I could see her juices. The thick penis went in easy enough as she lowered onto him, slowly and gently taking his huge tool. It eased in and was buried.

Then she rode him. She was filled and loved it. They fucked in the cowgirl position for at least twenty minutes. I mean up and down flailing about, his size no impediment. He was rock hard and she took all of him fully and with great enthusiasm. We ourselves never fucked with her on top. The size difference would not allow for much motion before I went soft and slipped out. Sara rode like the wind, moaning and enjoying the journey. She cried out, "This is so good, yes, I love this, fuck me baby fuck me good."

After her initial ride, they were far from finished. He rolled her over and started licking her sweet pussy. I walked around, filming the sex act and taking a few candid pics. Her cunt lips were exposed now and swelling. He was between her legs, and she was opened wide. Licking and probing her loins he dashed his tongue in and out of her, sending my wife in orbit. She clutched at his shoulders, wanting more. He eventually got up and positioned his prick to enter her sweltering opening once again. He sank deep into her as she moaned loudly, accepting his girth in full. She reached for his ass, and the two grabbed tight and banged in torrid unison. "You like this don't you?" he said. She proudly answered, "Oh baby yes; pound me, give it to me." This went on for nearly an hour. They finally took a break. Neither had come yet, and the night was just beginning.

I had gone through a whole SD card and DVD already; man this was nuts! Don was up for some extra athletic fun and took Sara to the nearby couch, where he sat her on top of him. She grabbed his glistening rod and again slid down his gigantic dark pole.

The melded together as, from far across the hotel room, I eagerly watched. She pushed her long thick blond locks back and bounced freely on his erection, impaling herself like never before on his truly large member. They fucked for another half hour, no lubrication necessary. This wife of mine could fuck! I was flabbergasted, yet not surprised. She was not getting this at home and it was a treat to behold.

They kissed and looked into each other's eyes, groaning with passion. They rose from the couch, and he placed her back on the bed, this time entering her in the man-on-top position. They pressed and screwed for another hour. During the missionary act, she played with her clit continuously and cried out in orgasm. Finally he was ready to cum. I got a bird's eye view from behind, waiting for the big moment. She said, "Pull out and take the condom off; cum on me." Finally, after hours of heated sex, he pulled out to get off. Sara's slit, now visible to me, was immense. Her pussy lips were so swollen and large, her gaping cunt hole so open, that I was in utter shock. He sprayed his jism all over her tummy. Some splashed onto her curvy breasts. He was moaning and sweating. Afterward they both collapsed in utter exhaustion. What an intense screw!

I suggested they take a quick shower together. They stood and walked, naked, to the bathroom. His cock was soft for the first time that evening, yet still massively thick, hanging between his legs. They disappeared into the bathroom to wash away hours of crazy sex. I thought to myself, *those two are so compatible sexually it isn't funny*.

Later on as we prepared to leave, they hugged and spoke of getting together again some night. We drove away with her completely satisfied sexually and saying that the night had been a fun and successful venture. "I would meet him again for sure," she proclaimed as we drove back home. It was great to meet a guy she liked who lived close by. This could really be a good thing.

The following week went by quickly. The holidays had arrived. We had a free day on Sunday and Don was aching to have Sara back in his arms. I mentioned that we could grab a quick sitter for an afternoon romp is she was up for it. She hesitated, saying she thought Tyron was next. I assured her we'd see Tyron soon—that scheduling was the only thing holding us back. She thought about it and finally said "why not?" to a second meeting with Don. This would be a first-time event—a second encounter was about to go down.

I admired Sara's new attitude. Here we were debating meeting Don again; Tyron would soon be just another hookup for us, too. She was a new person. When a sexual young woman is in heat and knows good sex is on the horizon, she prepares like no other. That girl ate healthier than ever. She worked out more and made sure her hair was taken care of with constant visits to the hairdresser and conditioning. She was in heat, literally, and it showed. Sara's body was the best I had ever seen it.

While online with Don, I mentioned how a prior phone conversation with Sara might help get her in the mood. Of all the buildup, she loved the flirting part best. I offered a few suggestions to make the afternoon meet up more exciting. I spoke with him early on the day of his call. "Don, why not ask her to fuck condom-less? Also ask if she'd like her ass taken." I made sure to mention that he should fuck her hard—I mean really make it wild, more rough. I had yet to see my wife sore from screwing, I mean man that would be cool. Sara actually sore; man that sounded weird! Another thing I mentioned was how about doing some positions she had never or seldom done—maybe a sideways sixty-nine, or her on top facing away, perhaps even on a table or someplace else original. He was up for the challenge and agreed on all of the above and whatever else he could dream up that might be new to her.

They chatted later in the day before the get-together, and I listened from around the corner to their phone conversation. "I can't do that; my husband and I have a deal that only he has me bare," was her first big statement. She giggled at the other things and agreed on most, saying she was excited now for the second chapter of their meet-up. We headed into Sunday afternoon, excited and ready for some fun.

Sara dressed sexy for the meet. Our friend from Florida had sent her some hot-pink panties—boy shorts with lacy edges. She slipped on a matching pink bra and pink fishnet stockings. She was smoking hot, covering the pink lingerie with a black mini-dress and accessorizing with wild platform shoes. It was cold so she put on a camo military jacket to tease her second-time lover.

We went to the same adjoining bar and hotel and sipped a few drinks before joining Don. This time we waited for him in the room itself; no introductions were needed. The hellos were few this time. He entered our suite, and they embraced quickly. They kissed wildly and began undressing fast and furiously. He slipped her out of her dress, revealing her new lingerie, and turned her about, admiring his prize— a young hotwife, firm yet sweet, sexy and very horny. As her husband, I was intent on watching over her, keeping her safe yet offering her to a bull with a larger sexual repertoire and a much bigger and already bulging hard-on.

She looked so good, so slim and in shape. He slid her new panties down and her mostly shaven bush made its first appearance. He stood and they kissed passionately again. She worked his belt loose, undoing his pants and letting them drop to the floor. He pulled his own shirt over his head.

She stood while her bull stroked his enormous cock. They slowly moved to the bed and sank down into it, holding each other tight. He moved her in a circle around him and into the sixty-nine position. She was surprised yet willing as he darted the tip of his tongue into her exposed cunt lips. She concentrated on his thick hard cock and flicked at his head with her tongue. She looked so sweet in her pink fishnets and painted fingernails to match. Her makeup was subtle and her lips, smudged with pink as well, had a soft glow. She was soon open enough and he dug into her soft mound of sweetness. She sucked his colossal prick and they were lost in foreplay.

Before too long she wanted him inside her, remembering the time before and long hours of deep dicking pleasure. She mounted him and again eased onto his shaft, taking him fully and smoothly. He was amazingly hard all night, delaying his own orgasm to the very end. He was a sexual machine for her. She rode him and cried out in pleasure, "I wanted this; I needed this."

He cupped her full breasts and tweaked her large swollen nipples. They fit perfectly, and she rode him like a wild cowgirl for what seemed over an hour. As they finally separated, he pushed into her from on top, passing his shaft deep into her and reaching around to grab her ass cheeks. As he thrust all thick nine inches into her fold, she took it all and grabbed his ass back, pushing and squealing all the while. They fucked hard and went on for quite some time before she cried out in orgasm. He rolled off of her, now panting, sweating and moaning. He was just getting started.

They took a little break, but she was far from finished. To arouse him again she danced about on the hotel floor, teasing and stripping to music on the radio. "Baby's Got Back" played on the radio, and she took great advantage of this tune and shook her bubbly butt to the music and to the pleasing view of her stud. His cock was up again, hard as ever, and he beckoned her to him. She teased more and kept out of reach. He liked what he saw and stood up to take her in his arms. My wife was ready to play, and he was too. She knelt on the floor and took him to a chair. Her mouth slid onto his hardness again as she sucked him silly. Her ass, now visible to me across the room from my place on the couch, was full, round and bouncing about. It was sight for the ages—what an ass, what a girl. Her swollen slit was gaping and wanting.

Still rock hard, he stood and led her to a nearby table. Pushing the drinks and whatnot off the table, he dropped her on its top. Things crashed to the floor. Looking deeply into his eyes, she winced as he parted her legs to expose her aching, swollen pussy. As he pushed into her, she cried out, "Oh yes!"

They moved to the bed again, and this time he had her get on top, facing away from him. This gave me a good view of her open cunt lips and swollen loins. His huge shaft pushed in and she rode him. They mated in unison and soon she could not help but touch herself, pushing away at her clit in orgasmic preparation. His shaft was so thick, so huge, her pussy so open, her labia major so split. She was getting very vocal, ready to explode. "Oh yes, oh my God, I'm going to cum!" she cried out. "Ohhhh, ummgh, oh, oh, yes, yes ..." They kept going, and she exploded again and kept going, ready to burst again. She bounced on him over and over; he was still hard and huge. He fit perfectly and she came again, screaming in lust. Soon he wanted to come, too. She jumped off him, grabbed his cock and stripped the condom away, stroking. She worked him into a frenzy until his cum was gushing all about.

Yet he was not through. They teased some more, lying sideways on the bed. They kissed and probed each other's necks, gaining momentum for more play. He was hard again in minutes and fingered her into wanting more, much more. Moving onto her, he deep-dicked into her moist opening, which welcomed him once more. This time he pounded harder, forcing his will into her. He held tight, driving his enormous cock deep into her. She moaned with pleasure and took it hard. He fucked her harder than anyone ever had. He made it a point to make her scream.

He cried out again in orgasm and they grasped each other tighter. It had been another three-hour screw session. Don had been rougher this time—that was obvious—and I liked it much more. My wife was mine to romance, mine to love. For him, she was a sexual friend, someone to fuck, to sexually pleasure, nothing more. He had done well. We said our goodbyes, and off we went. A new year was on its way.

It was obvious Sara had liked the sex, yet she made a point of mentioning that he had been rougher than the last time. I knew she missed the romance. In fact she got a little angry, saying that she missed Tyron and that it was really time for them to meet again. We argued some on the drive back, and at home during the following week. My excuses not to meet him had run dry and had no choice but to give in. Reluctantly I made a date to meet for a few months down the road. Tyron was eager to have my wife again; there was no denying that that fact. He made reservations himself for a place fairly close to our city. She was worth the long drive. When she heard about the arrangements, Sara's entire demeanor changed, and all was right in the household.

In the following weeks I kept an eye on the pics I had printed and the black dildo in the closet; there was movement almost every night. Sara was masturbating regularly now while awaiting the meeting with her top star stud. In the meantime, I scheduled an encounter with someone else for a month away at an amusement park out of town. A black guy I had been in touch with online had found a free weekend to hit the town for some fun. He was a sexy French fellow who I thought Sara might take a liking too.

I had also been in touch with a white guy who seemed cool. By chance, he lived nearby the park; I programmed him into my cellphone in case the other dude failed to show. My wife, who was fully focused on the Tyron get-together, was by no means thrilled by the prospect of any other encounters. She agreed, however, out of the need to escape from work and what not. Plus, she was soon to be reunited with her main squeeze; that thought excited her enough to make her willing to enjoy a Saturday night full of fun and mischief.

During the next month we fought a lot. Sara wanted more sex than I could provide personally or through our escapades. We had a serious talk about the future and how swinging may not be in the cards. We had had a few bad encounters that were still eating at her. The best ones—the ones she craved more of—were few and far between. We talked again about her having just one serious lover, a best buddy she could meet once a month. In no way could we agree on who that would be. I did not want some romantic trying to win her heart, and that was exactly what she wanted. So things were bleak. She wanted more sex, loving heartfelt sex, yet she wanted it to last for hours—for me to be so excited and hard that I could pound her non-stop. I needed fantasy and kinky words. I wanted her to be nasty and talk about the studs who satisfied her, to talk about what she wanted them to do. But in bed with me she spoke few words; all she wanted was closeness. We just could not find the right mix.

I envisioned us meeting many men and sharing many sexual adventures. I knew how young she still was and how her appetite for sex—once she rid herself of the guilt—was insatiable. She was still thinking deep inside that monogamy was the way to go, while suspecting that the only way to satisfaction was through swinging.

Shervay was to meet us that Saturday night. I could only hope Sara found him sexy. We needed a good night out, she needed sex, and I needed to see her happy. We met up at a small bar overlooking the beach, and at first glance I thought he was a good possibility. Sara, however, seemed disappointed. We sipped cocktails and chatted some; his French accent was not very noticeable. He was a talker, but not the flirty type that turned my little hotwife on. He seemed boring. I tried to make the best of it, as did my wife, but the encounter was going nowhere. They did not bond. Sara looked sexy in her tight jeans and snug-fitting blouse. We had a hotel room reserved nearby and the anticipation of a good connection still lingered in both our minds. Drinking was liquid courage for her, but even after a few drinks she was not into Shervay. We hit a dance club nearby and even that did nothing to get the night going. I told Shervay that Sara would not be up for anything else that evening, so we could free up the rest of the night for other attractions.

I called the white guy I had corresponded with online earlier in the week. Being nearby, Steve agreed to shoot over to meet us. The clock had struck eleven, and Sara was hesitant and growing tired. Steve took a while to arrive. I tried to keep Sara ready and excited, but she was losing interest quickly. When Steve finally showed up at the bar, he seemed somewhat cool. I hoped Sara liked his looks. He bought us drinks and chitchatted easily enough. Online he had mentioned he was very well endowed for a white guy and that was an exciting thought.

We hit the dance floor, and I separated from the two of them to give them time together. It was getting really late, and I figured it was now or never. When I returned Sara was not happy and ready to drive home. She was not interested in Steve and enough was enough for the evening. It was a rotten night, to say the least.

I had no other choice but to set up the Tyron meet as soon as possible. A date was set for the big second encounter with her favorite black stud. She was really upset though. These bad meetings had been so frustrating; I myself felt that perhaps our swinger days were coming to an end.

As the second date with Tyron drew nearer, my wife was more excited for a swinging trip than I'd ever seen her. She was working out constantly and eating so healthy I was amazed. She looked fabulous, never better. We shopped for new outfits, and she bought some really wonderful articles—including jewelry, special nail polish, and even a piercing that was a dangler just for Tyron to see. I found it all overblown. I thought, *At least she is wildly horny again and excited to swing.* The first time they'd met it had seemed rushed, although crazy successful. A second meet, better planned, could be hot. I just hoped he would lay off the whispering of sweet nothings and bang my little kitten the way she loved to ball. I mean, enough with the loving gestures; we were meeting for sex—nothing more, nothing less.

The day finally arrived, and she showered and sang in the bathroom. She gave herself the closest shave ever, leaving her sweet pussy almost bald. She put the silver dangling star belly piercing on, and man was it hot. A black skirt was laid on the bed, along with a very sexy red blouse. Her panties were side-tie red skimpy thong style and her bra a black pushup number. A pair of black high heels completed her wardrobe for the night.

We planned a dinner at a cool bar and drove the few hours to the meeting. I was uneasy on the drive, knowing that this guy was a real charmer, a gigolo in truth. You see, he had told me things I'd hidden from Sara ... how many wives and girlfriends he had bedded asked for him secretly without their partners' knowledge. How he'd had three hundred lovers and how Sara was in his top five. As he put it, she had a super personality. I laughed at that. Had he forgotten about her voracious sexual appetite? I kept thinking of all the times Sara had viewed the pictures that I'd placed on the top closet shelf of her and him engaged in various acts. I knew she constantly masturbated to them. Here at last was her big chance once again. She was giddy the entire ride.

We were the first to arrive at the small, secluded restaurant—more like a sexy bar than an eating hole. Sara had slipped a long red trench coat over her outfit to tease Tyron when he arrived. She was one hot ticket, a beautiful young voluptuous blonde. She was a woman on a mission, too, a mission for sex. After we'd waited a few minutes, I made my way to the bathroom, and when I came out, I spotted Sara running out the door into the parking lot. Outside I found her in his arms—hugging, smiling and blushing . "Oh dear," she said, "I missed you so much." This was weird—almost too weird—and I felt jealous for the first time.

We sat down and indulged in shrimp cocktails and chocolate martinis. The two of them locked eyes and flirted the whole time. I felt like an outsider, a true cuckold serving the couple before me. She was not acting like herself—tipsy already and laughing and joking and giggling. He knew all her hot spots, those within her brain. He fucked her mind. He made her anxious for more.

We made our way to the hotel. Tyron suggested Sara get acquainted with the suite and for us guys to go downstairs for a bit. She loved the idea and we headed to a sports bar on the lower level of the hotel. When we were alone—just us men—he made small talk to pass the time. We both liked sports, so that gave something to discuss. I made it a point to tell him to fuck my wife harder this time, to be more intense, try wild things make her go nuts. In my mind I was thinking, *enough with the whispers and sweet words of loving and the things that made her feel all warm and fussy*. I wanted this stud to pound my wife's oversized hole—to nail her silly.

After we returned, it took very little time for the two of them to embrace. He was a master of foreplay. His main weapon was the tease, and it sent my wife sky-rocketing. They nibbled necks, darted tongues, and looked in each other's eyes. I was getting bored already. For an hour they kissed, talked, and touched. No clothes were taken off.

I played some hip hop party music. Sara wanted it louder, yet I kept it low so I could hear their exchanges. This guy talked to her with so many words it was insane, telling her how nice she looked, how he loved her smile, how much she sparkled this evening ... *for God's sake, give me a break.* She ate it up, too. Slowly he slipped off her red blouse, and she gently eased him out of his button-down shirt. They kissed over and over, madly holding hands. Lovingly, he placed her on the bed and slid off her skirt, revealing her red side-tied bikini thong panties, her dandy body piercing and a body she had exercised regularly for just this very moment.

They rolled about the bed, kissing some more. I mentioned drinks, and he offered this in reply: "Why don't you go downstairs and have a drink? We'll be fine right here." I did not take that comment well. *What an ass, suggesting the cuck be gone and leave his wanton wife in Tyron's arms half-naked.* Tyron's lips licked at her big nipples now, dancing a jig around the protruding tips. He eased her panties down ever so slowly to reveal her already wet cunt. Her lips were full and swollen and juicy. He circled them and ate her pussy for almost an hour. She squirmed with delight and seemed dazed with desire, her eyes glazed over.

After he had finished showing off his oral skills, the stud took her in his arms and went back to the verbal seduction. I heard him say how he'd like to wake up with her in the morning and cook her a good breakfast. My camera battery was dying after the drawn-out foreplay, and he still had his pants on. Finally he made the move to remove his pants; he had held out for an hour, if not longer, in order to catch his prey in a web of seduction. He slid off his shorts, allowing his large prick to spring free, the mushroom head large and swollen. Sara grabbed his member and stroked it hard. After they kissed some more, Sara placed her mouth on his now stiff penis.

Gently she ran her mouth along the shaft of his member. She took him deep, and he moaned with delight. She sucked him up and down, the kind of blowjob that I had received from her maybe twice in our over ten years together. His bulging head jutted her cheeks open, urging her to open wider. She loved his bald pubic region, his shaven face, and his hairless balls. She pumped her mouth on him and he rose to full attention. But he would not come yet, although his thick cock was ever so ready.

They embraced again, laughing and playfully pressing into each other. He had her ready for more but was holding out on purpose. Sara wanted him, wanted him badly. I hoped she could not hold back, that she would mount him and ride him like a wild animal. But, the setting was more seductive, more erotic. He slid on a magnum condom and slowly positioned himself between her legs. They kissed and joined bodies as he delved inside her open, moist labia. She was soaked and open wide for him. He slid in fully and they melted together. When she looked up at him and said, "This is so wonderful, you have my spirit now. Make love to me," I nearly lost it.

They fucked for an hour in missionary. Then, finally, he did a little of what I had asked. He placed her doggy style on the floor, spanked her ass repeatedly, and fucked her hard—right on the hotel rug. That at least got me semi-hard. I looked on with more interest now. Afterward he pulled her to her feet, placed a chair against the wall and had her straddle him facing away. That, too, was interesting, but in time they again ended up in missionary, banging away, kissing all the while and whispering sweet nothings. She had an orgasm and announced how incredible it felt. They rolled around for many more minutes, teasing and fondling various body parts.

I had to speed up the action. I mentioned loudly that our babysitter could not stay late, that we needed to hit the road. I mean, hours of this was enough! He had not come and she knew it. Again she took him in her mouth and in a few moments he cried out in delight, shooting his wad into her small hand as she continued to lick his penis.

A second blowjob in one night. *Wow, this guy rated high.*

It was a while before we left the hotel. The two of them wanted more; they chatted and joked as I kept insisting we needed to leave. Even when we were outside he made his way to our car and talked more. After we drove off—much to my relief—Sara was at no loss for words. "Wow, that was awesome, so fun! What a great night." I listened to these rave reviews for miles and miles on the open dark road. I knew deep inside that I had seen the last of Tyron. I was through with him. She did not know it, however, and that was going to be the hard part. "Thank you so much honey," she said as we drove the long highway home.

Tyron's style did not suit my vision of a stud fucking my wife. He was too romantic, and dragged things out way too long. He was a player, and I did not enjoy his games. I would never allow him to meet us again. This was settled in my mind as we drove farther home. Sara, I'm sure, was envisioning many more such encounters. We were headed for showdown.

We battled for weeks thereafter. Our arguments never seemed to end. Sara wanted more of Tyron. However, she also began many discussions by saying that perhaps swinging was not for us. Our emotions were all over the place. On New Year's Eve we had a major fight. I had heard too much about how perhaps I should shave my pubic region, how she would like to spoon when we make love—a scenario that did not work in our case. With her round bubble butt pressing back into my hips, I was not long enough to reach inside her with my cock. It just would not work.

Next she said, "I'd like to see a new set of pics from Tyron and my last session." I made them for her, placing them with the old set on the closet's top shelf. It was never ending. I was chopped liver and her lover was fillet mignon. She sensed I was not into him. She was furious.

On New Year's Eve we went out and fought all night. I was feeling hurt and pissed at the same time. It had never been my intention to change the way Sara loved me, or see her lose her deep appreciation of all that we had been through as a couple and everything that goes along with a long marriage and having children. We had to iron things out and get a fresh start. If I offered up Tyron again, everything would be fine. That I would not do, yet I said no such thing. I was waiting until the moment was right.

Sara's idea of a fun night was to not always plan in advance. I liked planning. There were reasons to plan, especially at this time in our lives and in our swinging wife-sharing adventures. First off, we needed to find just the right guy. He had to be a flirt—young, good-looking, and fun to be around. Those were the qualities she demanded, and they were easy enough to find at a bar with her looks and sexy body. Yet, there were the other things that made me uneasy. Online I could screen men in advance, get a feel for them, perhaps have another husband or wife email me, tell me how their meeting with them had gone. Plus there was the hung factor that Sara did not address in her, "I want to just randomly go out to a bar and pick up a guy" plan. If the guys were small the connection would not work for crap. She liked to bang and get a good deep screw. There were way too many good-looking, fit, sexy, flirty guys with tiny little dicks out at bars and at the gym I went to that could not give her what she wanted. If I was sharing her, I wanted her ravished and taken control of. The times when a guy we met in a bar was small (and there were a few), she was in charge and he was overwhelmed. That sucked.

Lastly there was the danger factor. The idea of a random nut case was no thrill for me, either. With no prior screenings or recommendations, we might well end up with a freak. I could only imagine sweet little Sara standing nude with some psychopath pulling a gun and demanding shit, hitting her (or worse) out of fury. The random picking up of a hot stud in a bar on the spot just did not cut it in my book.

Chapter Nine

Almost another year passed, and then I had a plan. A new guy from out of state had popped up for a possible meeting. He seemed to fit the bill, and I came up with a plan of action. Recently at a party we'd met a cool couple who also liked black men for their female half. We had spoken about going out together some night and finding a bevy of black studs our ladies could choose from among and hook up with. They agreed to meet one night at a cool bar said to host many hot black guys.

Online I suggested to Blaine that he show up at the bar that very night. He would pretend not to know us. When we approached him, he was to act surprised yet interested. This in turn would fuel Sara's fantasy of picking up a random guy. If they hit it off, it would work great. He liked the idea and the plan was set in motion.

It was fun meeting Jim and Wendy, who had spunk. He was a great cuckold, yet like me, he enjoyed the ladies as well. His lady was a smoking older babe, late forties but built nice and horny as hell for the right guy. Just like Sara, black men turned her on. The bar we met at was dark yet had a nice cool feel to it. There were two sections, so we could have a nice dinner with cocktails on one side then go to the other and join the party. Sara looked sexy in a short brown skirt, tight white frilly blouse and a pair of sleek brown-and-gold high heels. Her bushy thick blond hair was teased just enough to give her that hot celebrity look. Wendy was hot, too. She had on a black micro miniskirt and a tiny red tank top blouse; I mean, she was a looker for her age. She, too, wore heels, real high heels that were black with silver bows. These two ladies were MILFs in every sense of the word tonight—hot kittens on the prowl.

A few drinks got the ball rolling and both ladies were loose and tipsy when the dancing began. There were a few guys who caught their eyes early on, too. Blaine arrived in good time, and he got the attention of the girls as well. Jim, not even knowing of my plan, went right over to him and invited him to sit with us. He was a hit right off the bat. He played it up, saying he was new in the area and meeting a friend for drinks. He was stocky in stature and dressed preppy, yet looked well. He had personality and both the women liked him. I was wondering if Wendy may want him as well. I was like, *what can we do here?*

As the night went on, more men arrived, more people danced, and the joint got hopping. Two more black dudes got in the mix, chatting with the wives and hanging close to us. One guy Wendy and Jim had met before; he was a looker, well-built and wearing lots of bling. Sara liked his looks, too. I figured either he or Blaine could work for a hotel room romp later on. The girls danced with the black men and Jim and I mingled about, looking for more possibilities. It was a new thrill to walk up to a random stud and say, *Look over there, that's my wife and she loves to fuck.* Some of the guys thought I was nuts, but a few smiled and asked questions. Jim was all over it and I hardly got a word in. He talked his lady up and offered her on a silver platter to most anyone black and handsome.

It was easier for him, he told me. Wendy was tight, her pussy small, so size was not a major issue—just looks and personality. They had it easy compared to Sara and me. Well Blaine and Sara hit it off and I asked her what she thought. She smiled and said, "I like him, he's cool, and I'd play with him."

So there we had it, a winner. Jim was okay with Wendy playing with the other stud they had met a while back—the one with the ruggedly handsome looks. He even pulled up a pic on his cellphone from a year earlier that showed them messing around together on a hotel bed—too funny but true.

We were going to meet in the same suite, all six of us, but Wendy's former lover was not ready to leave when we were. So we grabbed Blaine and took off for our hotel. Jim would call once they too left the bar, and we welcomed them all back to our suite whenever that time came.

Sara and Blaine were laughing and having a good old time when we hit the hotel room. I was glad to see that he was not shy and soon enough he embraced her with a hug and kiss. She was tipsy and horny and in no time they were making out. I got my video camera rolling and sat back for the show. I truly loved watching my sexy lass in action. She loved sex, and I liked her having sex.

The desire was there and they undressed one another with vigor. She was aggressive and got him on the bed. Now down to her thong and bra, she straddled him, and her hot bubble butt stole my camera angle and dominated the screen. Man, that woman had an ass to die for. They made out like wild animals, and he got naked by her helping hands.

I was thrown by his cock size. He was not that big. His pictures made it seem like he was much larger. But he was at least average and somewhat thick, so things were working out just fine. Sara was ablaze with passion, and before I knew it, she was pulling him into her missionary style for some quick fornication.

They pressed together and she groaned as he entered her warm womb. He licked at her aureole and sucked her big, protruding nipples. They kissed again and he fucked her harder and harder until she cried out in a libido-driven call of ecstasy. Soon she got on top of him, riding his dick. The gorgeous blond hair flowed down her back and that ass bounced in a yearning wantonness that heated up the hotel room, fogging my camera lens. My cellphone rang, and Jim said they would not be joining us, due to complications with the other black guy. I could not have cared less at that point. My wife was French kissing a stranger, and I had to focus.

She rode his dick up and down. Sara was lost in abandon, doing what she loved.

He was not through. After a break for bathroom duty, they again embraced, hugging and kissing and grinding together. He turned her over, wanting that ass, fucking that pussy, banging his balls into her fleshy, welcoming cunt.

Sara really loved the long session, the constant hard-on, and the passionate pounding. She proclaimed in a vibrant voice, "God, I love your cock!"

He did not stop; this call-out excited him. He pushed harder, spanked her ass, and got more vocal. She reached under to stroke his balls, then flicked and tapped her clit, coming loud, "Ohhhhh, ummm, yesssss!"

It was a hell of a session. Later she said it had been great. Yet I felt something had been missing. She had liked the sex, but her emotions had not been fully engaged. However, we left the hotel satisfied and said little as we drove back home.

In the coming weeks we met no one and barely mentioned swinging. She was constantly masturbating to the pics of Tyron and her together and using her black dildo. Every morning when I peeked on the shelf, the pics and vibrating dildo had been moved. I would adjust them in a new way each time only to see them rearranged from day to day.

"When can we meet Tyron again honey?" she would say. Those words rang again and again in my head over the next month. I lied, saying he was busy and out of town on work a lot. I knew we would never meet him again. I found myself trying to stay in decent shape. The nights when we went out and met men or attended parties made me want to look good. It may have been out of respect for Sara, or just that I wanted to feel better about myself. I hit the gym, ate better and groomed more than usual.

A former professional football player was going to be in our area the coming week. He was also a swinger and had answered our new personal ad. The ad read as follows:

> Happily married couple with sexy blond wife seek well-endowed handsome black stud for nights of passion and excitement.

Jerome was a big guy, 6'5 and nearly 250 pounds. He looked well-built, seeming to have low body fat and a decent sized cock. The one issue was that he was older than Sara. Then again, he was next door offering a clinic to the public. I mentioned to Sara, why not at least meet him for a drink? She agreed and plans were made.

She was not overly excited, I could tell. It was a work night and she was tired. Her attire was very casual jeans and a tight purple top. She was rushed and I sensed she felt pressured. After getting a last-minute sitter, we made our way to the guy's hotel room. Introductions were made. He had his head shaven and looked pretty good, and yes, he was a big guy but fit and personable. We left his room for drinks at a nearby place. He had on cargo shorts and a T-shirt, very laid-back.

Drinks were quick, nothing too grand—glass of wine for my dearest and a single beer for the football guy. He was retired but fairly well-known. He did a little flirting with the wife and teased her about going skinny-dipping. She seemed interested and I know liked the fact that he had been a sports star—even if it had been a while back.

Is it me, or are woman into the whole mind-fuck thing?

We decided to go back to his room and see if things could progress sexually.

Things sped up fast once inside his hotel room. He pulled his shirt off immediately and Sara was out of her pants before I had my camera out. She stood there, half-nude in a tiny pink thong and blue bra, looking up at this giant-like man. He pulled his shorts down, wasting no time, and stood there with no underwear on. He did, however, have a raging long hard-on that popped right up looking at my little wife. They moved together and he dominated the screen, taking her to the bed and laying her under him. He climbed high and held his long shaft over her mouth. His organ was about eight inches and semi-thick—nothing huge, but decent enough. She took him in her mouth and sucked him sloppily. He was lying sort of on top of her, forcing the action. Their size differential in body mass was incredible.

After getting some head, he wanted to fuck her. He quickly spread her legs and submerged his tool into her. She took all he had easily, with no extra lube. They pumped into each other's bodies—she, the small pale white wife, and he the big tall strong black ballplayer. She was lost under him but held her own. He gave it to her good, yet she took all he could give.

He wanted to move again and turned her to doggy style. He flexed his big muscles and Sara took his rod deep. There was no slow technique here. He pushed in and out hard, ramming her bubble butt firmly yet steadfastly. The romance was not there. I liked it. Sara seemed like she was going through the motions. So he got crazy and picked her right up off the bed and, standing, let her ride his stiff prick. This was a cool sight. The wife bounced with more vigor at least and got fucked in a new fun style. She enjoyed the variation, and after they landed back on the bed, she encouraged him to fuck her more.

He got back between her milky thighs and pushed in freely. She grabbed him, asking for more, and he moved faster, grunted and came. She was still aflame, and masturbated in front of us. She came wildly, crying out in joy. He wanted more, but she said she was tired. The party was over and she got dressed.

We said our goodbyes and on the way home she commented, "He was alright, nothing special but okay." I felt like overall, it had been disappointing. I had expected bigger and bolder things to occur. I mentioned it was time for another party at our friends Ted and Tia's. This time in my mind I would get some really great studs over to the place and we'd have a sweet party indeed. There could be no exceptions. It would have to be a costume party, a Halloween-type bash with all sorts of wild outfits and fun people. October 31st fell perfectly on a weekend night. In a few months we'd try again.

In the later part of the year, things came crashing down. We were not having much sex, work was stressful and times were hard. Sara made a new female friend at work. The two of them were spending time together and she had a new confidant. Late one evening, I was cleaning the cupboard and started going through some little papers in a small canister. One paper caught my eye. The only thing written on it was a phone number with an area code I thought I recognized.

I must make one thing clear at this point in the book: I am the person who sets up every meeting with anyone we hook up with. I have all contact information privately stored. All the e-mail addresses are hidden, and all phone numbers are concealed in private folders, password-protected and even coded to be recognizable to myself only. This piece of paper had an area code on it that had no reason to be hidden in this canister. I went directly to the contact list I had protected and secured for my eyes only. My hands were trembling. The number, as I expected, was his, yes, *his*. There was no way on earth Sara could have sneaked and got Tyron's number from me. I swallowed hard and became jittery. What on earth was she doing with his number?

My heart sank as I contemplated the situation. What was my beloved wife doing? Perhaps he had snuck it to her while they were meeting up the last time. But, why had she kept it and not told me? He would not do that. He knew I would not allow it. We both had agreed I should do all contacting for the three of us. I marched upstairs and, at near midnight in my now mad world, I awoke Sara and confronted her. I was both furious and heartbroken. She stumbled out of bed groggy, yet concerned. I knew things were nuts because she began crying right away.

Then my heart sank. Sara stuttered, "I, well, I ... got it from the cellphone bill. I wanted to call him, to see if he had feelings for me." I had forgotten all about the cellphone records. I fidgeted about, walking up and down the hallway. I went back to her and, looking her deep in the eyes, yelled, "Why on earth would you want to call him? I take care of all the setting-up stuff. You know that!" She cried and looked ashamed.

"This is our life, Sara. We have a family, a long-term marriage, and a history. Neither of us has ever stepped outside. We always lean on each other."

She replied in a soft voice, "I don't know why. I just wanted to talk to him, to see if he felt the same way about me as I did for him."

I was in shock again. I screamed, "ARE YOU FUCKING SERIOUS? What the hell were you thinking? He is not your boyfriend. He has hundreds of lovers and is enjoying you as one of many."

She looked at me sadly and said, "I'm so sorry."

I held my head in my hands, squeezing my temples tightly. I had lost a piece of my heart. My wife was looking to be a gigolo's lover and even sneaking about. I was to be left out of the loop and man, was I upset. This was not how it was supposed to be. It was all about *us*. I simply had a loving wife with greater sexual needs. She was my hotwife with a body that craved longer, deeper, and harder sessions. I had opened up our sex lives to the thrill of new adventure, the fun of going outside the norm as a couple—together through thick and thin.

What a mess. "I just can't separate the emotional part from the physical," Sara explained softly. "The sex with him was so passionate. I lose my mind when he embraces me. Our sex life was all I ever wanted. It may not be perfect but the closeness and emotional so-called spiritual factor for me always would override the physical." She did not know what else to say. I felt lost. All her orgasms, all her comments on what fun our little escapades had been were all crap. Why couldn't we just have fun sex meets? I had no intention of messing up her spirit.

There was really nowhere to go from there. I thought perhaps we were heading into more talks, but I was devastated and so was she. We dropped swinging again and tried to find some solace in each other. We put family first and stayed home a lot. I was bored and wondered if we could get back on track with at least a few hookups in the future. I let it go for some time.

The Halloween party we had planned was coming up, and Sara loved dressing up in costumes. It was only a party, and I would go on to tell her, we'd just go and have fun, no need to hook up with any guys or couples. We just needed to get out of the house.

The problem was, after the phone number debacle, she knew we'd never met Tyron again. She was thinking, *why go and meet anyone, why not stop cold turkey?* However, to satisfy me, and not make it into a Tyron-or-bust thing, Sara had no choice but to feign interest. I had no idea she had turned to her confidant at work. Her new friend was her ear for all our married-couple secrets. Sydney would listen to Sara everyday at lunchtime. Sara told her EVERYTHING! I had no idea about these conversations. I was, however, concerned that Sara was keeping secrets from me. Once I had found that phone number, my faith in her loyalty had crumbled. I would now check the cellphone bill myself. I would search her cellphone for texts and numbers unknown to me. I would constantly wonder if she had taken a lover on the side.

Halloween was one of Sara's fun holidays, and since we had helped arrange the party a long time back, she agreed to attend the bash. A constant debate went on in my mind these days. What was my role in this wife-sharing scheme? What did my wife really feel deep within? I knew that seeing her satisfied in bed was such a big turn-on that I could hardly imagine our life without it. I was myself constantly masturbating to the vids and pics I had taken of the encounters; they were all that could get me hard. I would be open to anything she really desired now. In truth, I guess more and more I was becoming a more traditional cuckold. She could probably demand anything of me as long I could see her nude legs spread and a hung guy making her moan.

There had to be a way to find better candidates. I searched for long hours looking for that perfect stud. I went out and bought Sara more sexy panties and g-strings that were so hot they burned. I picked up new bra and panty sets, lingerie, high-heeled boots, more thigh-high stockings, better belly-piercing styles, and more and more extra large condoms. I made sure she had new skirts, tops, and even invested in the new glass-made dildos for her pleasure. She was well equipped, to say the least. I gave her more sex, bought more Viagra. We discussed the cervix and how experts claimed that it had very sensitive nerve endings that would take flight when penetrated by a larger organ. I asked if she would prefer we meet couples only now. This would avoid issues perhaps.

She confided that the light-skinned guy named Don had even made comments that were "not right." I had never heard that one before. Other than Tyron, he had been the only guy we had met twice. I became interested in what he had said to her. She went on to say he offered to be her boyfriend if we ever split because she was so incredible. It was after the first time we had partied with him. He did not ask again the second time. For God's sake! I did not know that. All these swinging, open marriage wife swapping wife-lending situations packed too much bullshit. I, too, began to wonder if it all was worth the effort.

Before Halloween came, I managed to become online friends with a hot black guy from the Midwest. He was a very rugged dark-skinned dude with a big smile and even bigger dong. He had personality, was very funny, and I liked his style. To make matters interesting, he liked to fly, and was more than willing to fly into our home state and meet up. He and Sara would look incredible together. I set up a phone conversation one night, and they hit it off quite well. He made her crack up, and his English accent made her hot. His pictures online tickled her fancy, too. We had a great match in the works.

A date was set for an August weekend get-together. The idea was a Friday-night meeting and then another on Saturday, the day after. We had never done this before—a weekend fuck fest for my little baby doll. They got along well on the phone. I wanted my wife to be really into this unique set up. She loved the idea of a lot of sex with someone hot. We'd skip out Friday, getting a sitter, and on Saturday relatives could help out while we "went shopping." We would skip the shopping of course and meet again for an afternoon bang. I mean, he was traveling so far on an airplane that it was the least she could do—offer sweet pussy all weekend. Sara was excited and all for it.

As the weekend approached, a phone call was supposed to confirm the weekend's festivities. However, Marlow did not answer the call. We got his voice recorder, saying he was unable to come to the phone. I began to panic and kept calling and emailing. But we heard nothing. The weekend came, he never called and we were out of luck. Sara was like, "This is ridiculous. Why do we even try?" She had a point. When, days later, I made contact with Marlow, he said in his best English accent that there had been a flood in his area and he'd had to deal with a big mess. We did not know what to think. But, we never did meet the guy. Another excuse came up the following weekend—a baseball game for his son—so we just gave up.

I envisioned so many fantasies that could be fun for us to try. If there were no good studs that turned her on, we'd try new things and go in other directions. Sara, however, wanted just one hot guy. All my plans were not coming to fruition. I suggested we try a truck-stop setting, maybe some flashing on her part. I offered the idea of a glory hole, where strange cock came through hidden holes in booths. She could suck or fuck them without being seen. None of my ideas piqued her interest.

October finally arrived, and we put together costumes for the Halloween swinger's ball. Sara was going to be a sexy bunny. I was to be a gothic vampire. The party weekend came and I could only hope the darn single studs all showed up. We arrived early, and the hosts Ted and Tia were friendly as usual and welcomed us with open arms. Their place was amazing—decorated with great spooky yet sexy flair. As I said early, there were three floors, and the woodwork was beautiful. Sara tried on her bunny suit but decided it was not to her liking. She had brought along a superhero outfit as a backup and slipped into a spandex one-piece in no time. *Wow, that thing clung to her curves like magic glue.* The spandex was shiny black with silver sparkles all over it. Her ass popped out from the fabric, and her bosoms sprung out too. She put on long leather black boots to complement this black-and-silver superhero cat suit, and she was a knockout. The thing looked painted on her.

I, of course, had made sure to invite five hot single men to the party. This was a couples-only party, but the ladies would not complain if a few handsome single men mingled about. The problem was that none had shown up by the time most of the sexy guests had arrived. The music was loud, the drinks flowed, and everyone was having fun. These swinger-type Halloween parties are amazing. We charged the couples to attend and the pot was up to seven hundred dollars in no time. I told you these swinger folks had no concern for money when it came to fantasy and sexual exploration. Inhibitions are out the window and the woman dress so sexy it should be illegal—well, it would be at any other normal party.

A few guys finally popped in—one white fellow who looked okay and a black guy who I thought Sara may find interesting. People mingled about and sex was on everyone's mind. Couples went off to private rooms and some even played in public on the balcony overlooking the dancing guests. A few couples made advances to us. Men mostly would chat with Sara, hoping to get in her cat suit. The wives told me we should all join together for some fun. But, this was just not our thing, and Sara found none of the men really that great, other than that one black dude. The wife of one couple told me we should have a foursome—that I was sexy and her husband was immensely attracted to my Sara.

We were just not that interested in such a proposition.

The party moved downstairs to the open-room play area. We watched the couples making it all in the same room. Naked bodies writhed all about, and even the black guy Sara fancied was joining in. He offered his large, thick penis to a wanton Chinese-American wife who was thrilled with its size. He was also first to mount a black hotwife during our little watching period. Sara seemed disappointed that he had already given it up.

Later in the evening a friend of ours—a lovely woman called Jules—invited us to the loft. There she and her husband were entertaining another couple, and all of them were fondling her naked body resting on the futon. She was an attractive thirty-something lass, and this was her first breakout party. Naked, she spread her legs for the onlookers.

I touched her too, and man, I liked the fun. A hesitant Sara joined ever so slowly in touching her, and the black fellow from earlier in the evening made an appearance as well. Now Jules' husband badly wanted Sara. Earlier in the hallway, he had told me that she was so incredible in her costume he had a constant woody for her. Of all the wives, what a doll she was! He loved class—no tattoos, no overdone makeup, just pure beauty, and her hair, the hair of an angel. He said she was one of a kind.

He, however, would not get Sara. The black guy dressed like a pimp made his move. He fondled Sara from behind, touching her most sensitive parts. He wanted her, and she was sort of indecisive. The entire scene played out and we all kept fondling Jules, even as the guy behind Sara worked to slip her costume off. His fingers moved to her breasts and finally slid into her pussy. She was moaning, yet concerned that too many people were watching. It made her nervous. He pulled his large penis out for her, and the more she stroked it, the bigger and thicker it became. But she did not take the bait. She did not want everyone watching; it was too much attention.

I offered a suggestion: "Honey, would you like to take him to a private room where the three of us can have our own little party?" She looked at me with a horny yet stubborn expression. "I want him, but he was with all those ladies earlier. I'm no second fiddle, so tell him no." I took him aside and explained, and he dashed off without asking anything.

There was a young blonde at the party who Sara and I could not help but notice. She looked a lot like Sara and was a doll. The two of them chatted in the later part of the evening and actually shared a kiss. That surprised me. Sara even went so far as to say she was really attracted to this young lady, and that it would be fun to meet her at another party or privately some night.

The party ended eventually and we helped pick up before hitting the road for the drive back home. We wondered why we even went to those parties. Sara said, "I never find anyone good to be with."

I said, "It was still fun, right?"

She said it was but she felt like some sex should have gone down. Yet she did add, "It helps get us in the mood at least, right? You can do me good with we get home, honey."

I stopped at a gas station and popped my Viagra pill without hesitation.

We laid low in the months ahead. Sara was still thinking that swinging was not for us. There were just too many bad meetings when compared to the good. Now I knew that, with Tyron out of the mix, this would probably be her probable response to our future partying. I, too, was starting to think our days were numbered.

As time passed, I still had no idea that Sara had confided in her co-worker her experiences with swinging and all the emotions that went with it. Our lifestyle had always been just between us, for sake of our families, professions and the like. However, Sara had more building up then I realized when she talked with this younger woman during lunches.

Now, any typical twenty-something-year-old married woman would probably not approve of the idea of swinging, even more so of the idea of a wife who was shared with black men. Sara had told her she was debating stopping forever, but did not want her husband—good ol' me—to be mad or lose affection for her. She wondered now if we could ever have a real relationship—a monogamous lifestyle. They had been confiding in each other, unknown to me, for months. Much to my chagrin, her pal found swinging stupid, dirty, and horrible.

We celebrated Christmas and on New Year's Eve I suggested we meet someone.

I wanted to bring in the New Year in style. The best guy I could think of would be the light-skinned Don; his long lasting gigantic beer-can-thick prick was perfect for the job.

Sara debated the idea, but ended up saying, "You know what? I could use a great three-hour fuck, so let's go for it." So early New Year's Eve, we teamed up with our good friends Ted and Tia for bar-hopping. Don would meet us later on, and we'd meet at a hotel for the big deep-dick-pounding celebration later in the evening. I was so glad that rockets would burst and my little Sara would be satisfied.

Don called in between bars to say he was unable to meet. Something had come up, and he would be leaving the state as soon as possible. Sara took the news badly. She was mad, horny and upset. By then I was desperate to please her and ready to be the cuckold I thought I'd never become. I was willing to talk about my lack of sexual prowess and give her permission to randomly meet men. I even considered allowing her the freedom to go condom-less and consenting to eat her afterward. A cream pie was not on my list of fantasies. In the past I would never have gone anywhere near another guy's jism, let alone clean it up.

As we rode to another bar, these crazy thoughts lingered in my mind. The whole planning-to-meet a guy thing was not working out.

None of these thoughts mattered because, unbeknownst to me, our swinging days and my marriage were about to blow up in my face. As the night wore on, I had no idea that what was about to happen in the near future would rock my world.

We went to a few more bars, even hit a swing party. Couples were out in full force. We ended up hanging out at a bar, just the four of us. It was still fun, but there was no one she found remotely interesting. There would be no sex this New Year's Eve, and no satisfaction for either of us. The anxiety caused by our failure to hook up was killing us.

As the new year began, Sara was not open to any talk of swinging. She was not interested in another failure or taking a chance with anyone new. She was secretly talking about us with her co-worker, and she and this so-called friend was debating our lifestyle big-time.

Her friend heard only Sara's side, which left out anything positive and spoke only of her emotional pain, guilt, and concern for the future.

The woman, younger than Sara and recently married, could not understand how any man could share his wife. Her husband would be far too jealous. She told Sara, "He would kill a guy who even tried to hit on me."

Hearing this sort of talk day in and day out took a toll on my wife. She was convinced a monogamous relationship would suit her better. Having someone to back her up gave her the strength to confront me. I received a letter that spring. It was placed by my computer screen early one morning.

Dearest Derrin,

I've come to a point in my life and in this relationship that I must speak out. I am through with swinging. The person I have become needs security. I want to live a regular life. For many years I have tried to please you, to do what you wanted. I went along with these encounters to make you happy. But I can't separate the body from the spirit. I get way too emotional and it's killing me. I know that what I am doing is right for me. I feel, however, you will not be able to handle it. You like the thrill and the adventure too much. I love you, but if you can't live with my decision and be happy, then our marriage is over. I'm afraid that our marriage is done in any case.

—Sara

My world came to a sudden halt. I was at a loss for words. I sat in silence pondering what she had said. I loved her dearly; she was a great wife and a good mommy too. Here I was, almost fifty years old and forced to face a new reality. There had been so many signs that had led me to believe she loved the nights out. I know some of the encounters had turned out badly, yet others had been really exciting and she had seemed so into those ... The question was, could I live without them myself? In her letter, she might have hit upon the truth—that I couldn't handle a monogamous marriage.

Once one has embraced the cuckold lifestyle, the thought of plain sex minus the voyeurism is daunting. And Sara ... how could *she* ever go back to our vanilla sexual play? How would I ever satisfy her? I loved having a hotwife, but I loved Sara more. I wanted our family to stay together.

The choice was obvious; I would learn to be happy in a monogamous relationship. If Sara never took a lover again, I would be fine. We spent a long evening discussing everything. She finally admitted she had confided in a co-worker and that woman had given her the strength to come to the decision to never swing again.

I was not happy with that. *People talk*, I said. *She will tell everyone.* You will be looked down on and so will I. Our sexual life is no one's business but our own.

None of my ranting mattered. Sara was adamant about her choice, and that was that. We were done with the lifestyle. I was no longer to be the cuckold. I would have to carry the load and learn to satisfy my younger wife. Our marriage held together and months passed by.

Once things had settled down, a dangerous opportunity presented itself. I just had to mention it to Sara. A pro-athlete swinger was coming to our very town in two weeks. He was doing a clinic for a youth organization and he wanted to meet with us. He had made contact a year earlier; I had not initiated it. I had totally forgotten about him. He was younger than Sara, a current player, built to the max and very handsome; she'd go nuts over him. I debated whether to tell Sara about his visit.

I decided to let Sara know. If she said *no way in hell*, I would be fine. I had grown accustomed to the new normal. She in turn was getting used to going without outside sexual play. We were not having sex all that much, but I was trying hard.

I delicately explained the situation to Sara. "I know we have chosen to not meet any more men," I said, "however, a golden opportunity has arisen." She frowned at me and seemed very nervous. I took a deep breath and continued, "Way back, I mentioned that a star player was interested in you. Well, by chance, he is in our town next weekend and looking to hook up." I pulled out his online picture which I had saved and showed it to Sara.

The guy was a rock. He wore long, dreaded hair, was very tall and muscular and had a great-looking face. I was convinced that this type of guy would not let us down. If we had met him during our ten years of swinging, we would have never come to this devastating pass.

She studied his picture intensely. Her stare bore into my eyes. "I'll think about it," she said.

That was enough for me. This made me nervous. I could be fine with a "no" answer. I had no desire to fuel any more marriage-breakup thoughts. A few days later, Sara gave me her answer. "Just this one time, I guess ... I mean it's a one-in-a-million chance, and since he's right here in town, I'm okay to meet him." The stage was set.

Chapter Ten

I searched online to find the true meaning of the word, *cuckold*. I was curious if all my anxiety made sense, if I shared common ground with other cuckolds, or if I was way off base. This is what I found:

A cuckold, by simple definition, is a husband with a cheating wife. The husband could be willing or unknowing. I knew everything, and she was not cheating. This was all so confusing.

> The cuckold is a consummate voyeur ... who derives great pleasure from seeing his wife being pleasured and serviced by another male. Although he assumes a submissive role and will often assist during the course of the sex act, the "cuckold husband" may actually be the controlling, dominant party in the relationship. He may invite, encourage, and initiate the meetings.

It was a fact. I loved to watch. It was a huge turn-on and one of the greatest things I could ever witness. I also was the one to get things going, the plan-maker.

The Internet described these encounters as an "aphrodisiac," in that they enhanced the sex play between hubby and wife. The encounter could be revisited and replayed during subsequent love-making sessions.

> A cuckold husband is turned on by the idea of his wife having sex with other men. The cuckold husband attempts to convince his wife to embark on sexual flings, and if he succeeds, will then seek out a man who makes the most desirable partner (in the husband's view!) for his wife. In the case of a white cuckold husband, it is almost universal that a bigger, stronger,

exceptionally athletic (and possibly younger) black male will be considered as the most acceptable partner for the wife.

The above descriptions of cuckold were close enough to our situation. I realized that there were many other men like me. It was only logical: if the other male was bigger, stronger, more athletic, and possibly younger, the wife would receive maximum sexual stimulation, long-lasting intercourse, and get to enjoy many exotic positions during intercourse due to the greater strength and endowment of the chosen male. I agreed with all that I read.

I had to take into account what Sara was going through. The guilt was really upsetting her. She loved the sex, yet hated the anticipation of a bad encounter. Of course our biggest obstacle was not being able to separate the sex from the emotional baggage it entailed. The last thing I wanted was for her to be upset. This was supposed to be fun. I wanted us to experience all of it together, to use it to keep our sex life charged.

Since she had agreed to the meeting, Sara had become increasingly emotional and moody in all facets of her life; I did not know what to think. I was beginning to conclude that we should cancel.

More online research turned up a few good writings about the wife's point of view. According to research done by several psychologists, a woman tended to respond initially with "shock, dismay and revulsion" when her husband encouraged her to have sex with other males. She would also worry over whether her husband had lost interest in her sexually, or whether her husband was angry and looking to humiliate her, or whether her husbands no longer loved her and wanted to end her marriage.

At this stage the wife would usually reject the husband's requests completely and refuse to consider them further (in which case the husband had to give up and be satisfied with his fantasies or wait for the wife to get used to the idea). If she did show interest, it was rarely enthusiastic interest. Women almost always tried to hide any genuine excitement. Also, most women weren't comfortable with the idea of their husbands exposing them to judgment like some kind of prize heifer at the fair. It was all so confusing.

Friday night came at last. I told Sara sincerely that if she was not into it, we could still back out. She said, "Nope, let's do it. I feel fine with it."

We were to hook up at a local bar, and if things worked out, he had booked a hotel room down the road. Sara began getting ready. I was very interested in choice of outfits for the evening. After all, he was a star athlete and handsome—a big shot with good looks.

Sara put on a side-tie pair of light baby blue thong panties, a black push-up bra, and a white Victorian-type corset. Her skirt was long, lean, and sexy and her sandals jewel-encrusted. Her hair was longer than ever, almost touching the back of her ass. She looked stunning. However, I could feel her apprehension. We had met too many average guys, and those meets had been hell on our marriage. We lived in the boondocks, in a city far away from the hot nightlife, where men as a whole were beer-drinking duds.

We hit the bar and she sipped a Long Island ice tea, enjoyed it and asked for another. The guy we will call Travis called to say he was back from his clinic. He suggested we come to his hotel suite and join him. We had no problem with that and headed over.

The minute we stepped in his room, it was obvious this guy was something special. Travis was everything Sara could ask for—tall with long braided hair. He wore designer jeans and a sleek button-down blue shirt. He was, however, quiet. I tried to get a conversation going, but he was laid back and didn't pick up the thread. He had what she wanted. All he needed to do was flirt with her, tease her, and she would be his. Sara talked a lot and giggled, a sign she was interested. She, too, wanted him to loosen up.

I pulled out our iPod and mini speaker set and slipped on the "play list." The two of them finally got a little cozy. He got up from the bed, and from her place on the love seat, Sara looked up and smiled.

"So, what's up girl?" he said.

She waved a finger for him to come down to her level. There was a brush of faces as he leaned in. He pulled a chair up in from of my wife and sat in front of her. He teased her milky thighs—pushing her skirt up and fondling her ever so slightly.

She kissed him, and the temperature in the room rose. When he began to unbutton his shirt, Sara helped. They embraced and kissed passionately again. He probed his fingers between her legs, beneath her panty line, egging her on. She stood up, and he slid her skirt off. She helped him remove his jeans. He wore white athletic spandex boxers, very tight; his erection stood out. She wore her side-tie panties. They hugged.

Wow, what a sight she was with her ass sticking out as she leaned toward his muscular frame. Her hair cascaded down her back as they kissed again.

She slid her small hand into his shorts and stroked his manhood. Down his shorts went, and he brandished a larger then average, fairly thick penis.

He wasted no time taking my Sara to his bed. He slid her down and took her panties straight off. Her top soon followed, and there she was, naked and in heaven. He licked her pussy and she was in orbit. His big black body covered her tiny frame.

Travis was not a gigolo. He was ready to fuck. He did not draw out the make-a-woman-want-him foreplay, period. He must have had many women at his feet.

He put on a magnum condom and slid between Sara's legs. Sara grabbed his ass and pulled him into her. She cried out, "Oh God, you feel so awesome! So strong, so good." He was in shape and could fuck her with vigor. She was lost in the humping. He turned her over and did her doggie style. He wanted her bubble ass in sight and he pounded against it. Then he laid her on her back and entered her in missionary. He hammered her and yelled out in orgasm. It was one hot yet quick session. I had no doubt Sara was not ready to call it quits. He, however, rolled over and seemed happy.

Travis had used a condom, but he had come inside her. Lost in the session, she had forgotten to tell him to pull out. The last thing we needed in our lives was to worry about pregnancy.

After making his way to the bathroom to clean up, he returned quietly to the bed and lay back on his pillow. Sara wasted no time; she crawled to him and snuggled into his rugged body like a kitten. She nibbled his chest, and to my surprise, reached for his soft limp cock. She stroked it slowly, and he grew some. Before I knew it she had taken him in her mouth. The sucking had a purpose; my wife wanted more.

She got him hard. I wondered what would come next. Sara showed me—she climbed onto him, and her shapely ass glided down his shaft. Soon she was bouncing to the song, "Gold Digger," in which the chorus went something like "Get down, girl, get down." She was getting her groove on and fucking this star with total abandon.

After a good ride by my sexy wife, Travis took her in missionary and pounded her until he orgasmed again. Sara had not even gotten off yet. She was just getting started; Travis was done. He slipped his pants back on and then his shirt. Sara was obviously frustrated but, she, too, got dressed. They chatted some. He asked her who her favorite pro athlete was. She smiled and answered, "Well, you now, of course." I guessed it was time to leave, so we made our last goodbyes. Sara took him in a big hug and told him it had been awesome.

We chatted excitedly as we left the hotel—the husband and his hotwife discussing a just ended wild sexual romp. She said, "holy shit that was hot!"

I said, "Man, he was like a Greek god."

She shook her head in amazement. I brought up an issue that made me jittery on the drive home; she was off the pill as a result of our decision to end our escapades. Jesus I hoped that condom hadn't had a leak.

Little did I know this would be the very last time we would meet a substitute lover.

The final straw came a week later. The possibility of divorce was now on the table. Sara had again spoken at great length with her co-worker comrade. She was on edge. A pregnancy scare did not help matters. She came to me one afternoon, teary-eyed and upset. "Derrin, this is not going to work," she said. "I don't trust you anymore and I don't trust myself. I think this marriage is over. Everything I have done, I am ashamed of. If we stay together, this guilt will never go away. I need to start a new life."

My heart was pounding in my chest. I knew she was serious. We would go on to have many long talks. I still felt like I was losing her. I was losing my family, and man did it hurt.

I pointed out all the telltale signs that she had been enjoying our cuckold relationship. The many statements she made that indicated she had been having the time of her life. I admitted that many times it had not been good and that we had many bad choices, yet overall the lifestyle had seemed to suit her. She would hear nothing of it.

She explained again that her friend had given her the strength to embark on a new life, make a new beginning. She wanted nothing more to do with swinging or me; she wanted a divorce. I pleaded with her to calm down, but it looked as though she had made up her mind.

My fairytale notion of a cuckold fantasy—always so strong and perfect—was blowing up in my face. Reality had come to the table. Sara stated clearly, "Derrin, you can't live without this."

I contemplated the wreck of my marriage. I had two plain-as-day choices. One, I could let my marriage falter and lose Sara. I would get divorced and at nearly fifty years old begin again. Or, I could denounce swinging and promise her with all my heart that our past was just that. From then on we would embrace monogamy. I would let her know that I loved her dearly and she was more important than anything in the world.

To be honest I had no idea how either choice would work out. But, deep inside I knew I could not give up my wife of ten years or the family we had made together. The time had come to give up on our open marriage.

It took days and then months to convince Sara I was serious and could be happy with such a choice. I could only hope she still loved me. She was not pregnant; that was the first good news I had heard in weeks.

As the months went by I did all I could to reassure her. She noticed that I was really putting a lot into saving the relationship. She was right. I fought for it.

I have said farewell to life as a cuckold. Everything I wrote in my journals you have now read. It is all true. I'll never know how far I would have ventured onto the submissive side. The time had now come for me to live a normal life, whatever that means. This is not a Penthouse Forum letter, so in truth this tale does not end in some magnificent crescendo. As I end this book, I am still married and things are going well. No one really knows what the future may bring. I can only hope it's good for my wife and me.

The beginning ...

Made in the USA
Lexington, KY
11 October 2010